◀ 外研社翻译研究文库 ▶

译稿杀青！
文学翻译与翻译研究文集

TRANSLATED!

Papers on Literary and Translation Studies

（美）James S Holmes　著

外语教学与研究出版社
FOREIGN LANGUAGE TEACHING AND RESEARCH PRESS
北京　BEIJING

京权图字：01－2006－1009

Original edition published in English under the title *Translated! Papers on Literary Translation and Translation Studies*

ⓒ Editions Rodopi B. V., Amsterdam-Atlanta, GA 1994

图书在版编目(CIP)数据

译稿杀青！文学翻译与翻译研究文集 ＝ Translated! Papers on Literary Translation and Translation Studies / （美）霍姆斯（Holmes, J. S.）著 .— 北京：外语教学与研究出版社，2007.1
  （外研社翻译研究文库）
  ISBN 978－7－5600－6189－4

Ⅰ. 译… Ⅱ. 霍… Ⅲ. 文学—翻译—文集—英文 Ⅳ. I046－53

中国版本图书馆 CIP 数据核字 (2006) 第 154317 号

出 版 人：李朋义
责任编辑：唐 辉
封面设计：袁 璐
出版发行：外语教学与研究出版社
社 址：北京市西三环北路 19 号 (100089)
网 址：http://www.fltrp.com
印 刷：北京市鑫霸印务有限公司
开 本：650×980 1/16
印 张：8.25
版 次：2007 年 1 月第 1 版 2007 年 1 月第 1 次印刷
书 号：ISBN 978－7－5600－6189－4
定 价：12.90 元
＊ ＊ ＊

外研社翻译研究文库

专家委员会

（按姓氏笔画排列）

外研社翻译研究文库 *

现有书目:

About Translation P. Newmark
《论翻译》

A Practical Guide for Translators   G. Samuelsson-Brown
《译者实用指南》

Can Theory Help Translators? A Dialogue Between the Ivory Tower and the
Wordface A. Chesterman & E. Wagner
《理论对译者有用吗? 象牙塔与语言工作面之间的对话》

Corpora in Translator Education   F. Zanettin et al.
《语料库与译者培养》

Corpus-based Approaches to Contrastive Linguistics and Translation Studies
S. Granger
《基于语料库的语言对比和翻译研究》

Crosscultural Transgressions: Research Models in Translation Studies II,
Historical and Ideological Issues T. Hermans
《跨文化侵越——翻译学研究模式 (II): 历史与意识形态问题》

Electronic Tools for Translators F. Austermühl
《译者的电子工具》

Intercultural Faultlines: Research Models in Translation Studies I, Textual and
Cognitive Aspects M. Olohan
《超越文化断裂——翻译学研究模式 (I): 文本与认知的译学研究》

Method in Translation History A. Pym
《翻译史研究方法》

Text Analysis in Translation: Theory, Methodology, and Didactic Application of a
Model for Translation-Oriented Text Analysis (Second Edition) C. Nord
《翻译的文本分析模式: 理论、方法及教学应用》（第二版）

The Translator's Turn D. Robinson
《译者登场》

Translated! Papers on Literary Translation and Translation Studies   J. S. Holmes
《译稿杀青! 文学翻译与翻译研究文集》

＊ 本文库采用开放式结构，今后还将陆续添加其他有影响的翻译研究著作。

Translating Literature: Practice and Theory in a Comparative Literature Context
A. Lefevere
《文学翻译: 比较文学背景下的理论与实践》

Translation and Empire: Postcolonial Theories Explained   D. Robinson
《翻译与帝国: 后殖民理论解读》

Translation and Language: Linguistic Theories Explained   P. Fawcett
《翻译与语言: 语言学理论解读》

Translation and Literary Criticism: Translation as Analysis   M. G. Rose
《翻译与文学批评: 翻译作为分析手段》

Translation and Nation: Towards a Cultural Politics of Englishness
R. Ellis & L. Oakley-Brown
《翻译与民族: 英格兰的文化政治》

Translation and Norms   C. Schäffner
《翻译与规范》

Translation, Power, Subversion   R. Álvarez & M. Vidal
《翻译, 权力, 颠覆》

Translation Today: Trends and Perspectives   G. Anderman & M. Rogers
《今日翻译: 趋向与视角》

Unity in Diversity? Current Trends in Translation Studies   L. Bowker et al.
《多元下的统一? 当代翻译研究潮流》

Western Translation Theory: from Herodotus to Nietzsche   D. Robinson
《西方翻译理论: 从希罗多德到尼采》

霍姆斯（James Stratton Holmes,1924—1986）生于美国，1949 年起客居荷兰，直至故去。自 20 世纪 50 年代起，他一边以着装花哨的同性恋者的面目厕身荷兰诗坛，一边通过翻译将荷兰语文学——特别是荷兰语诗歌——介绍到英语世界。60 年代初，霍姆斯开始"认识到 50 年代预示着翻译研究革命的来临"。60 年代末，霍姆斯在供职于阿姆斯特丹大学普通文学研究系、同时兼职于阿姆斯特丹翻译学院之时，在进行诗歌创作、诗歌翻译和翻译教学之际，开始了对翻译理论的研究。1975 年，《翻译研究的名与实》（The Name and Nature of Translation Studies）一文在哥本哈根应用语言学年会上的宣读，使霍姆斯一鸣惊人。至 1988 年，《译稿杀青！文学翻译与翻译研究文集》（*Translated! Papers on Literary Translation and Translation Studies*）的出版，霍姆斯不仅为国际译界所瞩目，也为中国译界所关注。该论文集在国内的出版，正是应运而生的产物。

从互构语言文化学的角度而言，任何译学思想的形成与发展，除去语言载体形态的因素之外，往往也要受时代精神、民族（或地域）传统和个人特色三大文化要素交互影响制约，而前两大要素往往又体现在后一要素之中。因此，要探究霍姆斯在该论文集中所提出的译学思想，首先应关注霍姆斯作为译学研究者的主体特色，包括该主体特色所依托的时代的和民族（或地域）的文化背景。

若将霍姆斯的译学主体性特征一言以蔽之，即为：复合性，或拼合性。首先，从霍姆斯所处的时代文化背景来看，其译学研究复合或拼合了结构主义和解构主义、或者说现代主义和后现代主义两大时代文化阈限。上世纪 50 年代，他意识到翻译研究革命即将来临之时，西方译界以语言学为认知视角的结构主义认知模式正开始大行其道；而到 1968 年，他的译学研究成果最初面世时，解构主义思潮正在西欧特别是在法国风行一时；1975 年之后，他对翻译研究的一系列高屋建瓴的探讨，也与西方后现代主义的高潮形成了巧妙的际会。可以说，霍姆斯译学思想的形成和发展是跨时代的产物。其次，从霍姆斯所处的民族（或地域）文化背景来看，其译学研究也复合或拼合了北美实用主义主流民族文化传统和西欧低地国家非主流民族文化传统的分野。霍姆斯在 40 年代末从美国来到荷兰，这一跨民族、跨地域的生活经历，自然使其译学研究兼有北美和西欧两种民族认知文化传统的印痕。因此也可以说，霍姆斯的译学探究模式是跨民族、跨地域的认知模式的产物。再次，从霍姆斯本人的知识背景来看，他也成功地复合或拼合了直觉的、感性的和理性的各种认知主体性倾向。这主要体现在，霍姆斯不仅是一位"造诣非凡的文学艺术家"，而且是一位"头脑异常清晰的思想家"；不仅是一位成就卓然的翻译家，而且还是一位洞见独到的翻译理论家。一方面，其文学艺术家或诗人的艺术直觉不仅使他的译学研究"远离空洞的理论思辨"，而且其思想家的缜密求证也使他"远离自以为是的虚妄"；另一方面，他"作为翻译家的广泛经历"，使他"有可能时而将某些合宜的文字加诸翻译研究之中"，而他作为翻译理论家的理论研究，又"使他对翻译实践的可能态度的相关本质有着更深切的感受"。故而也可以说，霍姆斯的译学思想还是其自身复合认知结构的必然产物。由此可见，不同的时代文化因素，各异的地域文化因素，多样的个体认知主体性因素，都在霍姆斯身上达成了某种调和；而这种调和，又使他通过一个复合性或拼合性的独特视角，开拓了翻译研究的崭新视野。

霍姆斯以诗人、学者和翻译家三位一体的身份对翻译研究的关注经历了一个逐渐认识的过程。早在 60 年代初，身为阿姆斯特丹大学普通文学研究系讲师的霍姆斯，对"作为一门学科的文学翻译研究几乎没有任何兴趣"。到 60 年代末，他不仅"对文学翻译理论在文学研究领域所起的先锋作用有了充足的认识"，而且对语言学、文本批评和比较文学等新学科给翻译研究所提供的重要视角表示了密切的关注，由此也认识到了一场翻译研究革命的来临。从那时起，霍姆斯就以其特有的认知视角，对翻译问题开始了深入广泛的探究。该论文集所收录的论文就是他翻译研究（1968 年至 1984 年）的主要成果。

统言之，霍姆斯的译学研究理路有以下两个特征：第一，既从崭新的学科视角对翻译（特别是诗歌翻译）现象和翻译研究的古老话题进行了细致入微的观察，又借助旧有的有价值的翻译理论，对翻译研究现状进行历史视角下的阐释；第二，既从诗歌翻译的特定场合下对个人翻译准则或译法选择取向进行客观观察，以抽象出翻译技艺的通用范式，又以其高屋建瓴的理论视野在翻译理论思辨及翻译研究法方面进行了忠实的探索。在该论文集所收录的翻译研究论文中，霍姆斯的译学研究理路的这两大特征一目了然。

该论文集共收录霍姆斯在 1968 年至 1984 年期间发表的译学论文 10 篇，根据内容的不同，又可分为两部分：即"译诗部分"（The Poem Translated）和"翻译研究部分"（Studying Translation and Translation Studies）。"译诗部分"收录论文 5 篇，主要介绍了一些诗歌翻译家在诗歌翻译技巧方面的洞见。该洞见或由个人经验所致，或由理论研究所得，并转化为客观观察的更抽象的层次。其中第一篇论文《诗与元诗：论荷兰诗英译》（Poem and Metapoem: Poetry from Dutch to English）旨在洞悉译事奥妙，主要着眼于探究"诗歌翻译怎样成为复杂的决断过程的结果"。第二篇论文《诗歌翻译的形式和诗歌形式的翻译》（Forms of Verse Translation and the Translation of Verse Form）通过对诗歌结构形式的探究，对"文本"和"元文本"的核心概念进行厘定，旨在厘清诗歌翻译形式的混乱。在第三篇论文《诗歌翻译中的时间交叉因素》（The Cross-Temporal Factor in Verse Translation）和第四篇论文《重建波迈尔桥：论可译性的限度》（Rebuilding the Bridge at Bommel: Notes on the Limits of Translatability）中，霍姆斯旨在从文本分析的层面上解决"拟古"（to historicize）与"循今"（to modernize）的传统译学之争，并将文学翻译中的"自然倾向"（naturalizing tendency）与"异化倾向"（exoticizing tendency），同"保持原样的翻译"（retentive translation）与"再创造的翻译"（re-creative translation）的基本部分联系起来。第五篇论文《配制地图：从一个译者的笔记谈起》（On Matching and Making Maps: From a Translator's Notebook）对"翻译对等"这一传统翻译标准进行了颠覆性论证，指出"对等"并非是译者所应信守的译事圭臬。

该论文集的第二部分即"翻译研究部分"亦收录论文 5 篇，反映了霍姆斯对翻译理论研究的总体关注，并从方法论的角度对翻译范畴作出了有力的界定。除第一篇论文《论翻译研究的名与实》（The Name and Nature of Translation Studies）之外，该部分的其他论文探讨了与翻译研究有关的一系列思考，其要点表现在：一、翻译研究实质是"对翻译现象的描述和解释"；换言之，对翻译及其过程的描写（该描写没有合理的理论模式），是所有翻译理论必不可少的前提条件。二、对译作的研究必须关注"不同相关要素的相互关系"。三、翻译实践具有"提供有价值的洞见"和"成为检验假设的试金石"双重作用。总之，该论文集展示了霍姆斯在翻译研究领域的虽不完全但却非常忠实的多样化研究画卷。

霍姆斯在翻译研究中的开拓性贡献，主要体现在《论翻译研究的名与实》一文中，故需特别关注。该文理论意义的主要体现有二：一、对翻译研究作为一门独立学科的正名；二、对翻译研究学科的基本架构的规划。一方面，霍姆斯对翻译研究学科的命名提出了自己独到的见解。他认为，"Translatology"、"Translation Science"和"Translation Theory"等名称对翻译研究学科的界定要么太偏，要么太泛，皆不适合作为翻译研究学科的命名。随即他根据英语中新学科命名的习惯，提出了一个新的名词"Translation Studies"，作为翻译研究学科的命名。该命名提出之后，即得到国际译界某种程度的响应。除霍姆斯之外，以勒弗维尔（Andre Lefevere）、巴斯内特（Susan Bassnett）、赫尔曼斯（Theo Hermans）、斯内尔霍恩比（Mary Snell-Hornby）和图里（Gideon Toury）等人为代表的"翻译研究派"的出现，以及各大学翻译研究系（Department of Translation Studies）的陆续成立，即为其理论影响的明证。另一方面，霍姆斯对翻译研究学科的基本架构也进行了初步的规划。他首先将"翻译研究"（Translation Studies）学科分为"纯翻译研究"（Pure Translation Studies）和"应用翻译研究"（Applied Translation Studies）。前者又分为"理论翻译研究"（Theoretical Translation Studies）和"描写翻译研究"（Descriptive Translation Studies）。其中，"理论翻译研究"包括"普通理论"（General Theory）和"局部理论"（Partial Theory）的研究，而"局部理论"的研究主要包括"特定媒介理论"（Medium Restricted Theory）、"特定区域理论"（Area Restricted Theory）、"特定层级理论"（Rank Restricted Theory）、"特定文类理论"（Text-Type Restricted Theory）、"特定时间理论"（Time Restricted Theory）和"特定问题理论"（Problem Restricted Theory）的研究。"描写翻译研究"包括"产品取向"（Product Oriented）、"过程取向"（Process Oriented）和"功能取向"（Function Oriented）的研究。而"翻译研究"的另一大分支——"应用翻译研究"，则包括"译者培训"（Translator Training）、"翻译工具"（Translation Aids）和"翻译批评"（Translation Criticism）的研究。霍姆斯将翻译研究这门新兴学科的蓝图规划得如此清楚完备，开启了西方翻译学的学科性和系统性研究的先河。这一重大理论贡献，在西方译学界几乎无人堪与比肩。

研究霍姆斯，不能不提及董秋斯。60年代初，霍姆斯开始"认识到50年代预示着翻译研究革命的来临"的时候，董秋斯早在1951年就已提出要写一部《中国翻译学》的构想；1975年，霍姆斯在哥本哈根名声鹊起时，董秋斯的译学构想却被冷落殆尽；而时至今日，霍姆斯的译学思想在中国译界受到关注，而董秋斯创建"中国翻译学"的译学理念也同样得到了应有的重视。

但是，尽管霍姆斯的译学研究是客观的、抽象的、忠实的，并非意味着中国译学界就可以不加选择地生吞活剥之。前已提及，除去语言因素，时代、民族（或地域）和个人的文化要素也会影响和制约译学思想的形成和发展。例如，在西方天人相分、知行异道的文化传统下，霍姆斯自然得出"实践和理论永远都是不会相混"的译学观，这与崇尚"知行合一"的华夏认知传统无疑是相悖的。又如，霍姆斯《论翻译研究的名与实》一文的面世，勾勒出了翻译学发展的总体蓝图，这是西方民族理性认知的传统使然；而董秋斯并未对"放之四海而皆准"的翻译学大道进行细致入微的逻辑推论，只是对带有地域色彩的"中国翻译学"的研究理路约略提及，实为"道昭而不道"、"大道至简至易"和"大道可执而不可说"的华夏认知理路的自然展现。总之，只有在特定的东西方文化背景下，合理的吸收和科学的借鉴才能成为可能。因此，读者在学习研究霍姆斯的译学思想之时，既应把握中西译学发展的不同理路，也应关注中西文化发展的不同传统，如此方能相得益彰。

孟凡君　北京师范大学外文学院博士

辜正坤　北京大学外国语学院教授、博士生导师

Table of Contents

Introduction by Raymond van den Broeck   1

Part One: The Poem Translated   7

1 Poem and Metapoem: Poetry from Dutch to English   9

2 Forms of Verse Translation and the Translation of Verse Form   23

3 The Cross-Temporal Factor in Verse Translation   35

4 Rebuilding the Bridge at Bommel: Notes on the Limits of Translatability   45

5 On Matching and Making Maps: From a Translator's Notebook   53

Part Two: Studying Translation and Translation Studies   65

6 The Name and Nature of Translation Studies   67

7 Describing Literary Translations: Models and Methods   81

8 Translation Theory, Translation Theories, Translation Studies,
   and the Translator   93

9 The Future of Translation Theory: A Handful of Theses   99

10 The State of Two Arts: Literary Translation and Translation
    Studies in the West Today   103

Index of Names   113

Introduction

The publication of the present collection of essays and papers by the late James S Holmes (1924-1986) is an event that has a double importance. It is important first because the author's observations on translation, in particular that of poetry, and on the academic study of translation and of translations, previously presented over a period of about fifteen years (between 1968 and 1984) in a wide range of periodicals and on a variety of occasions, are now brought together in a convenient and accessible form. Secondly, it is important because this over-all view provides the interested reader with a very faithful reflection of the developments that, during the period in question, have taken place in theoretical thinking about translation and in the methodology of translation studies. The importance of this second point will be appreciated when we consider that between the 1960s and the 1980s this discipline has progressed from its difficult beginnings to experience an unprecedented expansion.

Among the translation scholars known to me, James S Holmes always held a privileged position. This arose from the exceptional range of his talents: he was a gifted literary artist as well as a remarkably clear thinker in his academic field. I should like to say a little more about this two-sided quality of Holmes' personality. He was in the first place a poet with a voice of his own and a highly personal subject-matter; the fact that he quite soon put his poetic talent at the service of the other poets whose work he translated had partly to do with the fact that he left his native America in the late 1940s for the Netherlands, which was to become his second homeland, the country where he was to spend most of the rest of his life. Even so, he retained his U.S. citizenship, which made it easier for him to spend, at regular intervals, periods in his distant native land. A participant in two cultures, at home both with their languages and with the literatures written in those languages, he was thus the ideal mediator between the Low Countries and the Anglo-American world. Modern Dutch poetry, in particular, won international attention through his translations. His excellence as a translator received official recognition both in the Netherlands — where he was awarded the highest distinction for literary translators, the Martinus Nijhoff Prize, as early as 1956 — and in the Dutch-speaking part of Belgium — where in 1984 he received the Flemish Community's first Triennial Prize for the translation of Dutch literature. In the Low Countries he counted many poets among his friends. Together with Ed. Hoornik and Hans van Marle he was the driving force of the periodical *Delta: A Review of Arts, Life, and Thought in the Netherlands* (1958-1973), in which he published translations of almost all important Dutch and Flemish poets. He also translated such Latin poets as Catullus and Martial, being attracted in particular by the homo-erotic element in their work. Not least, he wrote poems of his own, at one moment under the transparent pseudonym of Jacob Lowland (using bound verse), at another moment under the more familiar name Jim Holmes (using free verse). Of his epic *Billy the Crisco Kid,* a narrative poem in *ottava rima* intended to comprise ten cantos of 800 lines each, he was alas not even able to complete two cantos.

James Holmes had, without doubt, a passion for translating poetry. It was not merely, as in the first years, a way out of the impasse of a poetic activity of his own that still had to find its own vision and its own forms. It was, far more, the expression of a character trait common to many translators, which Holmes defined, in an interview he gave in 1984, as "something in the introverted type that greatly enjoys being a mediator".

Alongside Holmes the creative artist there was also Holmes the literary scholar, with whom we are here chiefly concerned. It would however be wrong to discuss the latter without having first given some account of the former. Even though Holmes himself admitted, in the interview already referred to, that when he began to look into theoretical problems he found it necessary to divide himself "rather schizophrenically" into the practicing translator on the one hand, the theoretician on the other, one can see in him a distinct interaction between these two personalities. "It has been my extensive experience as a translator", said Holmes, "that has made it possible for me to contribute the occasional sensible word to translation studies." At the same time, the study of theory made him more aware of the relative nature of possible attitudes towards translation as praxis. While in the literary theory of the 1950s and '60s many of those who wrote about literary translation were inclined to take their own way of translating as the norm for how everyone should translate, Holmes quite soon was to perceive that when it came to the theoretical study of the craft the best thing one could do was to detach oneself as far as possible from one's own working rules and personal choices in particular translational situations. In his case, then, practice and theory were never confused, and never distorted each other; on the contrary, their fruitful interaction at once guarded the scholar from sterile theorization and the translator from vain complacency.

When in the 1960s Holmes became a lecturer at the Department of

General Literary Studies of the University of Amsterdam (a post he continued to hold until a year before his death), there was as yet hardly any interest within this field for the study of translated literature as an academic discipline. Any such subject was at that time even regarded as somewhat revolutionary — which may have been an added attraction for Holmes, who never had any use for established social values or rigid, institutionalized points of view.

By the late 1960s he had sufficiently familiarized himself with the literature of translation theory to be able to play a pioneering role in this area of literary studies. He realized as did few others that the 1950s had heralded a revolution in translation studies. He knew that the new disciplines whose practitioners were beginning to concern themselves with the various aspects of the phenomenon of translation could provide this discipline with important insights. Yet at the same time he remained deeply convinced of the importance of familiarity with the history of translation and translation theory. Since he was of the opinion that the present could be explained only with reference to the past, there was scarcely any worthwhile past contribution to translation theory that escaped his attention. The library he virtually built up from nothing at his department in Amsterdam strikingly demonstrates that solicitude. In the series *Approaches to Translation Studies,* of which he was the founder and until shortly before his death the general editor, appeared two very important historical studies (Nos. 2 and 4: T.R. Steiner, *English Translation Theory 1650-1800* and André Lefevere, *Translating Literature: The German Tradition from Luther to Rosenzweig*). Works for which he himself took direct responsibility included the first English translation of Estienne Dolet's *La manière de bien traduire d'une langue en aultre* (*Modern Poetry in Translation,* No. 41/42) and, under the title "The Essential Tytler", an abridged version of A.F. Tytler's *Essay on the Principles of Translation* (*MPT*, No. 43).

At the same time Holmes remained alert to every new development in linguistics, textual criticism, or comparative literary studies that concerned translation and the study of translation. As a regular participant at the world conferences of the Applied Linguistics Association and the International Comparative Literature Association, he knew that in both fields translation and translations regularly came under discussion. The diversity of points of view and methods that accompanied such discussion did not disturb him; he saw them, rather, as an advantage in that they led to the object of study being considered in greater depth and in greater breadth. Even so, he often thought it a pity that attention given to translation remained in this way somewhat fragmented, and this stimulated him to strive for appropriate channels of communication by means of which translation scholars could more easily exchange views concerning the results of their researches. He thus made plans for an international journal of translation studies, for years published a *Newsletter*, and founded the series *Approaches to Translation Studies*. Reliable and friendly as Holmes was in discussion, he established a great number of international contacts through the many conferences, colloquia, and symposia he attended. Many will for instance have met him at one of the world conferences of the FIT (International Federation of Translators), at which time and again he was the spokesman for those who advocated a scholarly approach to translation and translation studies. I myself had the good fortune to meet him for the first time in 1968 during the International Conference on General and Applied Linguistics at Antwerp. Through him I met, that same year, the Slovak translation scholar the late Anton Popovič, who was on an academic visit to Amsterdam. Some years later Itamar Even-Zohar (Tel Aviv) spent some time in Amsterdam at Holmes' invitation. These contacts made possible a fruitful collaboration, whose results are to be seen. A succession of three international colloquia, at Leuven (1976), Tel Aviv (1978), and Antwerp (1980) respectively, were the direct result of these contacts. If not the driving force behind these high-level academic encounters, Holmes' certainly provided the inspiration behind them, and much experienced advice. The group of translation scholars at present gradually becoming internationally known, from the circuit Amsterdam-Anwerp-Leuven-Nitra-Tel Aviv, can with a certain pride call itself Holmes' progeny.

The present collection presents a faithful though, alas, incomplete picture of Holmes' multifarious activities in the field of translation studies. This is particularly the case of the first part (The Poem Translated), which could in fact be considered as complete only if it were accompanied by its necessary complement: the translated poems themselves. Let us hope that it will not be long before these valuable texts are published in collected form. This part introduces us to the poetry translator who tries to share with his colleagues insights into his craft acquired through both personal experience and theoretical study, transferred to a more abstract level of objective observation. The topics are in fact age-old, but are here given original expression. The first essay offers the reader the opportunity to take a look into the translator's secret workshop and to see for himself how the translation of a poem comes about as the result of a complex process of decision-making (Jiří Levý is here a constant background presence). In the second essay the author succeeds in bringing order into the chaos of possible modes of translation as applied to the original verse text, by means of a structural model in which the paired concepts text/metatext occupy a central place. The third and fourth settle the traditional dichotomy of "to historicize" *versus* "to modernize", by placing the problem on levels of text analysis on which also naturalizing *versus* exoticizing tendencies in literary translation can be linked with the fundamental option between "retentive" and "re-creative" translation. The fifth essay makes clear, among other things, why the notion of "translation equivalence" is in fact, if taken literally, not a reliable criterion.

The second part of this collection reflects the author's unflagging concern to secure an independent academic status for his field, and to define within it methodologically well-grounded lines of force. The first essay, in particular, is one that provides a lead in this direction, and is innovative, especially when one considers when it was written. I know of no other contribution to translation studies in which the methodological problems faced by the young discipline are explained so clearly and so completely. I should like to draw the attention of readers to a piece that complements this essay: Holmes' bibliographical contribution to the volume *Literature and Translation* (Leuven, 1978), a well-considered survey in which, true to himself, he puts into practice the classificatory principles he had expressed in the essay in question. The other essays and papers in the second part pursue the train of thought thus begun: translation studies, with its claims to describe and elucidate the phenom-enon of translation, and translations, stands a chance of success only in so far as translation scholars are aware of the interrelations of the various components involved. That is to say that the description of translation and translation processes is an indispensable precondition for all theorizing; that description, in turn, cannot manage without plausible theoretical models; and that the practice of translation, finally, is assigned a double role: it provides valuable insights, and it is the touchstone by which hypotheses are tested.

This volume is dedicated, in respectful posthumous homage, to the late James Stratton Holmes. It is recommended to readers as a continuing reminder, or else a refreshing introduction, to the thinking of a man who not only did pioneering work in his field but whose views on translation will continue to stimulate future generations.

Raymond van den Broeck

6

For a selective bibliography, see Scott Rollins, "Publikaties van James S Holmes", *PEN Kwartaal* (Amsterdam), No. 62/63 (December 1986/January 1987), pp. 39-41.

Part One:
The Poem Translated

"Poem and Metapoem: Poetry from Dutch to English" is the revised text of a paper presented at the International Conference on General and Applied Linguistics held in Antwerp, 22-24 April 1968. First published in *Linguistica Antverpiensia* (Antwerp), 3 (1969), pp. 101-115. A Slovak translation was published in *Romboid* (Bratislava), 1970, No. 5, pp. 7-12.

Poem and Metapoem: Poetry from Dutch to English

However fierce the discussion may rage regarding the precise limits between prose and poetry, this much can surely be said: that while the tendency of much prose is towards univalence at the rank of the word and redundancy at the rank of the message, the tendency of much verse, and particularly modern verse, is towards multivalence at word rank and information (in the cybernetic sense of unpredictability) at message rank. To put this in another way: when we read prose we have an inclination to expect a single, precise over-all message, unambiguous in meaning, and in trying to grasp that meaning we will strive to attribute to each semantic unit one single significance that seems most obvious or most logical in the context; when we read verse, however, the form itself serves as a signal to us that our minds should remain open to ambiguities at every rank, and even once we have chosen one specific signification[1] of a word, a line, a stanza, or an entire poem as the chief surface signification, we do not reject other possible significations out of hand, but hold them in abeyance, as so many further elements in the highly intricate communication which we expect a poem to be. In this most complex of all linguistic structures, a whole range of significations, and not simply the signification most obvious or most logical, fuse to create the total 'meaning' and the total effect.

Similarly it is possible to make a rule-of-thumb distinction between some of the basic problems involved in translating prose and those involved in translating poetry. A root problem of all translation is the fact that the semantic field of a word, the entire complex network of meanings it signifies, never matches exactly the semantic field of any one word in any other language. It is primarily for this reason that, on the ideal level, all translation is distortion, and all translators are traitors. On the level of practical efficiency, however, the translator of prose is usually able to bypass this obstacle. True, with every word he deletes possible meanings of the original and inserts new possible meanings into the translation. But since most of those meanings in the original were screened off by their context, and since he in the same way screens off most of the possible meanings of the words he selects, the result, if the translator is skilled and talented in his craft, is an astonishing goodness of fit between the original and the translation.

Because of the quite different way in which poets use language, the person who sets out to translate verse is faced by a much more complex problem. It is not surprising, then, that while the general theorists of translation have tended to define the central problems of translating in terms of arriving at "equivalence",[2] those concerned primarily with verse translation are inclined to despair of any such thing.[3]

Indeed, since Croce's pronouncement, two-thirds of a century ago, that translation of a literary work of art is impossible in any absolute sense,[4] there has been a long train of such prophets of despair. One of the more recent is Gottfried Benn, who in 1951 roundly declared: "Man kann das Gedicht als das Unübersetzbare definieren...".[5]

And even those critics concerned with analysing verse translations have tended in recent years to abandon the older method which tested each detail of the form and substance of the translation against the measuring stick of the original, in favour of analyses of the original and the translation as two distinct structures each in its own right: structures in some way linked to each other, it is true, but in various explications by little more than the scar of a severed umbilical cord. It would seem to be worth our while to consider a third approach to the problem of verse translation, one which steers midway between the unattainable ideal of equivalence and the desperate counsel of impossibility. Over against the creative literature of poetry, fiction, and drama, in which the writer makes use of language to formulate certain statements about matters, situations, and emotions which are themselves usually extra-linguistic (in short, about what might, with some hesitation be called "reality"),[6] one can distinguish a body of "meta-literature",[7] writing which makes use of language to communicate something about literature itself. Literary criticism and explication are obvious examples of such meta-literature, but so, too, is literary translation.

The poem intended as a translation of a poem into another language, which as one type of meta-literature we may call a "metapoem",[8] is from this point of view a fundamentally different kind of object from the poem from which it derives. This difference is perhaps best defined in the following proposition: MP : P : : P : R
— the relation of the metapoem to the original poem is as that of the original poem to "reality".

The relation of metapoem to poem is in this regard similar to that of an analysis or explication of a poem to that poem. In either case the author, whether as metapoet or as critic, is making a comment about the original poem, and as he tries to clarify what the poem is doing, what it is about, he inevitably falls into the fallacy of paraphrase, shifting emphases and distorting meanings, since the poem is "a verbal object whose value is inseparable from the particular words used".[9]

There is, however, a major difference between the metapoet and the critic in the *type* of commentary they make about a poem. The critic interprets by analysis, and can allow himself, if he wishes, many times the length of the original poem in order to make his analytic interpretation as explicit and complete as his limitations will allow. The metapoem, on the other hand, interprets, as William Frost has pointed out, not by analysis but by enactment.[10] Unlike criticism, but like the original poem, it, too, "strives to be a verbal object whose value is inseparable from the particular words used".

It is frequently said that to translate poetry one must be a poet. This is not entirely true, nor is it the entire truth. In order to create a verbal object of the metapoetic kind, one must perform some (but not all) of the functions of a critic, some (but not all) of the functions of a poet, and some functions not normally required of either critic or poet. Like the critic, the metapoet will strive to comprehend as thoroughly as possible the many features of the original poem, against the setting of the poet's other writings, the literary traditions of the source culture, and the expressive means of the source language. Like the poet, he will strive to exploit his own creative powers, the literary traditions of the target culture, and the expressive means of the target language in order to produce a verbal object that to all appearances is nothing more nor less than a poem. He differs, in other words, from the critic in what he does with the results of his critical analysis, and from the poet in where he derives the materials for his verse.

Linking together these two activities, the critical and the poetic, is an activity which is uniquely the metapoet's: the activity of organizing and resolving a confrontation between the norms and conventions of one linguistic system, literary tradition, and poetic sensibility, as embodied in the original poem as he has analysed it, and the norms and conventions of another linguistic system, literary tradition, and poetic sensibility to be drawn on for the metapoem he hopes to create. This activity of confrontation and resolution is, as the late Jiří Levý pointed out,[11] an elaborate process of decision-making, in which every decision taken governs to some extent the nature of all decisions still to be taken, and the appropriateness of each decision must be tested in terms of its appositeness within the emerging structure of the metapoem as a whole.

It is these three factors — acumen as a critic, craftsmanship as a poet, and skill in the analysing and resolving of a confrontation of norms and conventions across linguistic and cultural barriers: in the making of appropriate decisions — that determine the degree to which the metapoet is capable of creating a new verbal object which, for all its differences from the original poem at every specific point, is nevertheless basically similar to it as an overall structure.[12]

The problems involved in resolving a confrontation of the kind I have just mentioned may vary greatly in emphasis according to the languages and the cultures concerned. In what follows I shall attempt to identify some of the impediments to appropriate decision-making in the process of creating a metapoem in one specific language, English, on the basis of a poem in another specific language, Dutch. A first major impediment is one that is common to all translation between closely related languages. Let me illustrate it by an example not from Dutch, but from German. In the opening line to a familiar poem, Goethe asks, "Kennst du das Land, wo die Zitronen blühn...?" Much of the effect of this line lies in the characteristically Goethean combination of the exotic image of lemon trees in blossom with the straightforward syntax of everyday interrogative speech: "Kennst du das Stück, das jetzt im Theater spielt?" "Kennst du das Haus, das gestern verbrannt ist?"

Semantically the line presents few problems for the English translator, and a dynamic rendering into prose of an equivalent register might be: "Do you know the country where the lemon trees blossom?" or "Do you know the country of the blossoming lemon trees?" In poetry, however, "the temptation", as Jackson Mathews has pointed out, "is much greater... than in prose to fall under the spell of the model, to try to imitate its obvious features, even its syntax..."[13] And even, he might have added, when formally similar syntax has a quite different function, or a dysfunction, in the target language. Those who have attempted to render Goethe's "Mignon" into English verse have repeatedly fallen into the trap which this line opens for them, and "Kennst du das Land..." time and again becomes "Knowst thou the land..."[14] Syntactically and morphologically the two passages are close parallels, yet the shift in the total message conveyed is tremendous. The interrogatory inversion instead of an auxiliary construction with "do", the use of the old second-person singular forms for the verb and the pronoun, the translation of German *Land* as "land" in place of "country": all these elements combine to lend the English passage the wan, archaic quality of a dead poetic tradition, far removed from the colloquial vigour of the German.

There is a frequent tendency of this kind when the source and target languages are closely related. A type of linguistic interference, it may manifest itself in such features as the matching of form to form regardless of meaning, the intrusion of source-language vocabulary and syntax in the target language, and the contamination of semantic areas,[15] and the result is often a mechanistic translation at the lowest ranks, without the preliminary operations of poem analysis and interlinguistic confrontation. In memory of those translators of Goethe, I have sometimes referred to the phenomenon as the "citric syndrome." But whatever we may choose to call it, it is a phenomenon that repeatedly stands in the way of satisfactory translation from Dutch to English.[16]

A second impediment to appropriate decision-making in Dutch-English verse translation is one that is particular to translation from little-translated languages. Professor Rabin has called attention to the fact that the more and the longer translations are made from language A to language B, the easier it becomes to translate from A to B (though not, it should be noted, in the reverse direction). This fact Rabin attributes to the accumulation of what he calls a "translation stock," a collection of proven solutions to specific problems that frequently arise in A-to-B translation. This translation stock, once developed, may be passed on for centuries, or it may die out rapidly as A-to-B translation dwindles.[17]

Such a translation stock is clearly available for the translator from English to Dutch, since a long and continuous tradition of translation in this direction, for a wide variety of purposes, has led to the development of a large number of practical solutions to translation problems and the creation of a certain degree of consensus regarding "right" and "wrong" renderings. This is much less the case for translation from Dutch to English. True, there is a fairly long tradition of Dutch-to-English translation within the Low Countries, and a stock of solutions of a certain kind has accumulated. But these solutions, the work of generations of philologists and schoolmasters with one specific aim in view, are largely unsuited to the needs of translation in any genuine sense, as distinguished from translation as a didactic method presumed to impart and test linguistic skills. On the level of literary translation, the translator from Dutch to English has almost invariably had to start from scratch, working outside a tradition and finding his own solutions as he went along. This has been particularly true in the case of poetry, where there has never been anything even approaching a tradition of translation in the Dutch-English direction, solely the work of scattered individuals, isolated in time, place, and readership. Only in the past few years has this situation begun to change, as more Dutch poetry than hitherto has been published more widely than heretofore, in translations by more English and American metapoets.[18]

A similar impediment to appropriate decision-making derives from the position of little-known literatures. Concomitant with an absence of a translation tradition is a lack of knowledge of the literary background against which a poem translated from the Dutch should be read when it appears. A rendering into English of a poem by Georg Trakl or Apollinaire falls into (or perhaps contradicts) a general pattern of German or French poetry already available to the English poetry reader. A rendering of a poem by, say, Paul van Ostaijen must stand by itself, isolated both from the remainder of Van Ostaijen's work and from the entire body of Dutch poetry. This means that the translator of a poem by Van Ostaijen has to approach his task in quite a different way from the translator of Trakl or Apollinaire.

How he approaches it is determined to some extent by yet another set of problems, those that are specific to the translation of poetry into English, from whatever language. Some of these problems are fairly constant, and have to do with the nature of the English language; I shall mention three of them.

One is the fact that English contains an extraordinarily high proportion of monosyllabic words, a proportion that moreover is highest of all among the words most frequently used. A second problem, partly a result of the first, is the shifting, loose accent of English, which for the poet makes various metres all but impossible, and others possible only by dint of a high degree of tension between hypothetical metre and actual rhythm. A third problem is the dearth of true rhymes. Levý, who made comparative studies of rhyme material in various languages, pointed out that for instance the English word "love" rhymes only with "glove", "dove", and "shove" (or combinations of these words with prefixes), plus, by a poetic licence born of sheer necessity, such words as "cove", "Jove", and "wove", or "move" and "groove". Italian, in contrast, has a large repertoire of words available to rhyme with the various forms of *amore*.[19] Each of these three linguistic facts constitutes a formidable obstacle to any attempt at carrying over outward form from the foreign poem to the English metapoem.

Other problems, more bound to one specific time, have to do with the expectations of readers for poetry in English. As Reuben Brower has indicated, "The average reader of a translation in English wants to find the kind of experience which has become identified with 'poetry' in his readings of English literature. The translator who wishes to be read must in some degree satisfy this want."[20] Must satisfy it, that is to say, even though the poem he is translating, conforming as it does to the kind of experience which has become identified with poetry in another literary tradition, may be of a quite different nature. How restrictive that want may be is exemplified by a recent statement of W.H. Auden's:

...my own conviction is that in this age poetry... can no longer be written in the High, even in the Golden Style, only in a Drab Style... By a Drab Style I mean a quiet tone of voice and a modesty of gesture which deliberately avoids drawing attention to itself as poetry with a capital P. Whenever a modern poet raises his voice he makes me feel embarrassed...[21]

To accept Auden's criterion out of hand would mean to decide that much of contemporary Dutch poetry (including most of the verse of the Generation of the Fifties), as well as much of the finest Dutch poetry of the past, from Vondel to Verweij, either cannot at all be translated for this generation, or can be translated only by a kind of inverse alchemy, transmuting the gold into baser metal. Fortunately not all discerning readers of poetry in English are quite so restrictive in their demands. Yet the fact remains that the metapoem, if it is to achieve an effect as a poem in English, must satisfy certain requirements that may be alien to the original poem, and the metapoet has the choice of yielding to them, abandoning his translation, or keeping it in his drawer until the taste may change.

A few of the problems that come to the fore during the attempt to transform a Dutch poem into an English metapoem may be illustrated by two examples. The first is an English rendering of a poem by the contemporary Flemish poet Paul Snoek.

"Rustic Landscape"

The ducks are like our cousins:
they waggle and walk
and slavering at the mouth
in the mud grow old.

But all at once a terrific
bang almost breaks
their pleasant peasant membranes.

That was the farmer himself of course:
he's trying the shotgun out,
the lout. He cut an apple
in the snout and cried, stark red
with relief: "I'm dressing,
yes, a golden pear."

And did those quacking cousins have a laugh.
(1) They prune their roses
with a crooked knife;
(2) How old are the ducks?[22]

This is not the place for a detailed comparison of the English text against the Dutch original, Snoek's "Rustiek landschapje",[23] but even a cursory reading of the two texts in conjunction is enough to uncover the major decision-requiring problem. A fundamental theme of the Dutch poem is the juxtaposition of *ganzen* (geese) and *onze tantes* (our aunts), with such descriptive terms as *waggelen, wandelen, worden... oud,* and *kwakende* applying to both. These juxtaposed and coalescing images (suddenly separated again in the two "clues" which close the poem, turning it into a picture puzzle) are reinforced acoustically by a complex system of alliteration and internal rhyme.

A low-rank translation of the opening line would yield "The geese are like our aunts" or a similar rendering. But that lacks the acoustic complexity of the Dutch. Moreover it leads the translator to the further problem that in English geese do not quack (see line fourteen) but honk or possibly hiss. Retention of the geese leads to honking relatives, and that to a suggestion, disturbingly inappropriate in this context, of honking car-horns. Retention of the quacking, on the other hand, leads from geese to ducks. A choice for ducks and quacking instead of honking and geese opens up the possibility of turning the aunts into cousins and so to beginning the metapoem with the initial elements for an acoustic system parallel to that of the Dutch ("De ganzen zijn net onze tantes..."; "The ducks are like our cousins..."). This choice, however, leaves the human image less concrete at the end of the first line than in the Dutch, since cousins, unlike aunts, are of unspecified sex and relative age; the translator who has given preference to this series of choices must rely on the rest of the first stanza, reinforced by the last, to make it clear that the cousins, too, are female and growing old. In other words the major cluster of choices facing the translator of this poem is that of either reconstructing the acoustic qualities of the Dutch at the cost of shifting the nature of two of the poem's major images (though preserving the nature of their juxtaposition) or retaining the images at the cost of introducing alien implications with the "honking"[24] and failing to parallel the acoustic qualities of the poem.

The second translation reflects a similar problem of choice between emphasis on the aspect of sound and the aspect of image. But in the case of this poem, Hubert van Herreweghen's "Avond aan zee",[25] the factors governing the choice are quite different. Where in "Rustiek landschapje" the nature of the relationship between the two juxtaposed images was central, not the precise nature of the images themselves, in "Avond aan zee" the emphasis is squarely on an image as such: that of a sow as metaphor for the evening sky as the sun sets in the sea. In a poem of this kind any shift even in subordinate imagic details can be quite precarious. On the formal level, Snoek's poem is highly individual, contained in an organic form developed for this poem and it alone; Van Herreweghen's poem, on the other hand, is formally quite traditional: five four-line stanzas rhyming *abba* (stanzas one, two, four, and five) or *abab* (stanza three), each line with six (masculine-rhyme lines) or seven (feminine-rhyme) syllables and three accents. The sole unorthodox elements in the form are the rhyming of *zinkt* with *zingt* in stanza three[26] and the somewhat uneven rhythm throughout.

Such close adherence to traditional form is more common among contemporary Dutch poets (at least in Flanders) than among their English and American counterparts, and there is little reason for the translator to concentrate on reproducing a familiar poetic form at the cost of introducing major shifts in the imagic material of the poem. On the other hand, by expanding the incidental use of consonance in the Dutch poem into a basic formal principle of consonance and assonance in the English metapoem, while at the same time admitting two-accent lines alongside the three-accent of the original, the translator can create a form for the English metapoem which has two important advantages. Situationally, it is actually more closely equivalent to the Dutch than a correspondent form would be. And it has the flexibility to provide a close fit for the semantic and imagic material of the Dutch poem. The result is an English metapoem which is formally quite different from the Dutch poem but in every other way follows the original with a minimum of skewing.

"Evening by the Sea"

An evening of olives;
a lemon sky
surfaces its belly
on a green sea.

A sow lying on its side
grumbling and dangerous,
a belly of thwacking light,
teeth gleeful with rage.

From here to where the earth
slopes away and sinks,
the gigantic red-haired beast
flames and flashes and sings.

Vicious mother with lips
of froth across yellow teeth,
eyes of a lightning white,
asquint with ruttish tricks;

belly, your teats hang there
maternally light and full,
plenty of milk for all.
Evening licks our desire.[27]

Notes

1. Using the term 'signification' in its largest sense, to include not only the semantic function of a linguistic unit, but also its other functions (acoustic, rhythmic, etc.) within the poem.

2. In the sense of Catford's "textual equivalence" or "translational equivalence" as opposed to "formal correspondence", see J.C. Catford, *A Linguistic Theory of Translation* (Language and Language Learning, Vol. 8; London: Oxford University Press, 1965), Ch. III, pp. 27-34. There is unfortunately not the least consistency in terminology among translation theorists. Nida, for instance, uses the terms "equivalence" and "correspondence" more or less interchangeably, and his "dymanic equivalence" and "formal equivalence" have meanings somewhat different from Catford's terminological pair: see Eugene A. Nida, *Toward a Science of Translating, with Special Reference to Principles and Procedures Involved in Bible Translating* (Leiden: Brill, 1964), Ch. VIII, pp. 156-192.

3. There have always been theorists voicing this point of view, but only in this century would they appear to have gained ascendancy. This ascendancy would seem to parallel the contemporary acceptance of the critical position that form and content are one, and the message of a poem inseparable from the words conveying it.

4. Benedetto Croce, *Estetica come scienza dell'espressione e linguistica generale. Teoria e storia* (Bari: Laterza, 11th ed., 1965 [1st ed. 1902]), Parte Prima, Ch. IX, pp. 75-82.

5. Gottfried Benn, "Probleme der Lyrik", *Gesammelte Werke*, 1 (Wiesbaden: Limes Verlag, 1959), pp. 494-532, quotation p. 510. Benn's position is almost identical with that of Robert Frost, who once defined poetry as that which cannot be translated.

6. "Reality", that is to say, in the sense in which many literary critics use the term; the sense in which Roland Barthes writes of "the world": "... a novelist or a poet is supposed to speak about objects and phenomena which, whether imaginary or not, are external and anterior to language. The world exists and the writer uses language; such is the definition of literature." "The object of criticism", Barthes goes on to say, "is quite different; it deals not with 'the world', but with the linguistic formulations made by others; it is a comment on a comment, a secondary language or *meta*-language..., applied to a primary language (or language-as-object)", Roland Barthes, "Criticism as Language", *The Times Literary Supplement* (London), 27 September 1963 (special "Critics Abroad" issue), pp. 739-740, quotation p. 739. (The essay was reprinted in French in Barthes' *Essais critiques* [Collection Tel Quel; Paris: Editions du Seuil, 1964] under the title "Qu'est-ce que la critique?" [pp. 252-257, quotation p. 255]. Cf. also his earlier note "Littérature et métalangage", *Essais critiques*, pp. 106-107.)

7. This seems to me a more appropriate term than Barthes' "metalanguage", and has the advantage of avoiding confusion with other meanings of "meta-language" and "metalinguistics" in contemporary usage.

8. After having written this paper I realized that the term metapoem had previously been used in a somewhat different sense, more or less synonymous with the traditional meaning of "imitation": see John MacFarlane, "Modes of Translation", *Durham University Journal* (Durham), 45 (1952-1953), pp. 77-93, esp. p. 90.

9. William Frost, *Dryden and the Art of Translation* (Yale Studies in English, Vol. 128; New Haven, Conn.: Yale University Press, 1955), p. 16.

10. *Ibid.*

11. Jiří Levý, "Translation as a Decision Process", in *To Honor Roman Jakobson: Essays on the Occasion of His Seventieth Birthday* (three vols.; The Hague: Mouton,

1967), II, pp. 1171-1182. Cf. Levý, *Umění překladu* (Prague: Československý spisovatel, 1963), p. 148; Anton Popovič, "Translation Analysis and Literary History: A Slovak Approach to the Problem", *Babel* (Avignon), 14 (1968), pp. 68-76, esp. p. 73.

12. The views expressed in the first part of this essay were developed further in a paper presented at the conference on literary translation theory held in Bratislava late in May, 1968 and printed in the proceedings of the conference, James S Holmes with Frans de Haan and Anton Popovič (eds.), *The Nature of Translation: Essays on the Theory and Practice of Literary Translation* (Bratislava: Publishing House of the Slovak Academy of Sciences and The Hague: Mouton, 1970), under the title "Forms of Verse Translation and the Translation of Verse Form" (see pp. 23-33 below).

13. Jackson Mathews, "Third Thoughts on Translating Poetry", in Reuben A. Brower (ed.), *On Translation* (Harvard Studies in Comparative Literature, Vol. 23; Cambridge, Mass.: Harvard University Press, 1959), pp. 67-77, quotation p. 67.

14. See the translations listed in Lucretia Van Tuyl Simmons, *Goethe's Lyric Poems in English Translation prior to 1860* (University of Wisconsin Studies in Language and Literature, Vol. 6; Madison: [University of Wisconsin], 1919), and in Stella M. Hinz, *Goethe's Lyric Poems in English Translation after 1860* (same series, Vol. 26; 1928).

15. Cf. Irène C. Spilka, "On Translating the Mental Status Schedule", *Meta* (Montreal), 13 (1968), pp. 4-20; esp. p. 13.

16. One striking example may emphasize my point. A few years ago the following text was published in the authoritative American review *Poetry*:

"The Old Man"

An old man in the street
his small story to the old woman
it is nothing it sounds like a thin tragedy
his voice is white
like a knife that so long was whetted
till the steel was thin
Like an object outside him hangs the voice
over the long black coat
The old meager man in his black coat
seems a black plant
You see this stasps the fear through your mouth
the first taste of an anaesthetic

(translation Hidde Van Ameyden van Duym; *Poetry* [Chicago], 104 [1964], p. 175). There is some remarkable English here. A reading of the Dutch poem by Paul van Ostaijen on the facing page of *Poetry* shows why:

"De oude man"

Een oud man in de straat
zijn klein verhaal aan de oude vrouw
het is niets het klinkt als een ijl treurspel
zijn stem is wit
zij gelijkt een mes dat zo lang werd aangewet
tot het staal dun werd
Gelijk een voorwerp buiten hem hangt deze stem
boven de lange zwarte jas

De oude magere in zijn zwarte jas
gelijkt een zwarte plant
Ziet gij dit snokt de angst door uw mond
het eerste smaken van een narkose

(Paul van Ostaijen, *Verzameld werk: Poëzie* [two vols.; Antwerp: De Sikkel, The Hague: Daamen, and Amsterdam: Van Oorschot, (1952)], II, p. 244).

One can see the lexis and syntax of the original Dutch constantly breaking through the surface of the English, across the barrier of language. At the rank of lexis, a *klein verhaal* is equated to a "small story", an *ijl treurspel* to a "thin tragedy", *mager* to "meager", and *de angst* to "the fear". At a higher rank "Gelijk een voorwerp buiten hem hangt deze stem" is rendered as "Like an object outside him hangs the voice", and "zij gelijkt een mes dat zo lang werd aangewet/tot het staal dun werd" as the contamination "like a knife that so long was whetted / till the steel was thin". The last line of the poem but one is particularly unclear in the English, partly perhaps because of what may be a misprint, but primarily because the translator has depended on lexical translation to solve his dilemma for him, instead of making a choice between two readings ("Ziet gij dit / snokt de angst door uw mond" or "If/When you see this fear quivers through your mouth", and "Ziet gij / dit snokt de angst door uw mond" or "You see, this sucks the fear through your mouth"). The result is that, by retaining the syntax of the Dutch, he has created a line which must be read either as approximating the less probable of the two Dutch meanings ("You see / this stasps the fear through your mouth") or as meaningless ("You see this / stasps the fear through your mouth").

A translation of this kind, though presented formally as a poem, becomes rather a comment on the general nature of Dutch syntax than a comment on a specific Dutch poem. Indeed, the deviations from the syntactic norms of English stand in the way of an appreciation of the English text as poetry. (This is not true of all kinds of syntactic deviation, of course. But there is apparently a fundamental difference in effect between the deviations from the norm of "translationese" and those of "poetic licence".)

17. C. Rabin, "The Linguistics of Translation", in *Aspects of Translation* (The Communication Research Centre, University College, London: Studies in Communication, Vol. 5; London: Secker and Warburg, 1958), pp. 123-145, esp. pp. 144-145.

18. More Dutch poetry was published in English translation during the single decade 1955-1965 than in all the preceding years of this century taken together.

19. Jiří Levý, "Die Theorie des Verses — Ihre mathematischen Aspekte", in Helmut Kreuzer and Rul Gunzenhäuser (eds.), *Mathematik und Dichtung, Versuch zur Frage einer exakten Literaturwissenschaft* (Munich: Nymphenburger Verlagshandlung, 1965), pp. 211-231, esp. p. 220; cf. Levý, *Umění překladu*, pp. 194-197.

20. Reuben A. Brower, "Seven Agamemnons", in Brower, *On Translation*, pp. 173-195. quotation p. 173.

21. W.H. Auden, "The Mythical World of Opera" (T.S. Eliot Lectures, 1967), *The Times Literary Supplement*, 2 November 1967, pp. 1039-1040, quotation p. 1039.

22. My translation. First printed in *Delta: A Review of Arts, Life, and Thought in the Netherlands* (Amsterdam), 8, No. 2 (Summer 1965), p. 49.

23. "Rustiek landschapje"

De ganzen zijn net onze tantes:
zij waggelen en wandelen
en worden watertandend
in de modder oud.

Maar plots doet een geweldig
knalletje hun landelijke,
liefelijke vliezen bijna scheuren.

Dat was een hereboer natuurlijk:
hij schiet met loden spek,
de gek. Hij sneed een appel
in de bek en riep spierrood
van ontspanning: "Ik mest,
jawel, ik mest een gulden peer".

Of die kwakende tantes moesten lachen.
1. Zij snoeien hun rozen
met een kromgekweekt mes;
2. Hoe oud zijn de ganzen?

(Paul Snoek, *De heilige gedichten, 1956-1958* [Antwerp: Ontwikkeling and Rotterdam: Donker, 1959], p.39).

24. There is of course also the literalist's alternative of retaining both the quacking and the geese, at the cost of confusing the image and tearing the fabric of the poem.

25. "Avond aan zee"

Een avond van olijven,
een hemel van citroen,
komt op een zee van groen
met zijn buik boven drijven.

Een zeug die op de zijde
grommend gevaarlijk ligt,
een buik vol kletsend licht,
tanden van woede blijde.

Ver tot de hellende aarde
onder de einder zinkt,
het vlammend rood behaarde
groot beeest dat blinkt en zingt.

Wrede moeder met schuimen
lip over geel gebit,
ogen bliksemend wit,
loens van bronstige luimen,

buik, moederlijk daar hangen,
uw tepels licht en melk,
zatheit van dronk voor elk.
Avond likt ons verlangen.

(Hubert van Herreweghen, *Vleugels* [Hasselt: Heideland, (1962)], p. 52).

26. Since Van Herreweghen is Belgian, perhaps also the rhyme *ligt – licht* should be considered consonance rather than *rime riche*.

27. My translation. First printed in *The Literary Review: An International Journal of*

Contemporary Writing (Teaneck, New Jersey), 7, No. 3 (Spring 1964: special Flanders Number), p. 466.

"Forms of Verse Translation and the Translation of Verse Form" is the revised text of a paper presented at the International Conference on Translation as an Art organized 29 and 30 May 1968 in Bratislava. It first appeared in *Babel* (Avignon), 15 (1969), pp. 195-201, and was reprinted in James S Holmes et al. (eds.), *The Nature of Translation: Essays on the Theory and Practice of Literary Translation* (The Hague & Paris: Mouton, and Bratislava: Publishing House of the Slovak Academy of Sciences, 1970; Approaches to Translation Studies, 1), pp. 91-105. A Polish translation was published in *Literatura na świecie* (Warsaw), 1977, No. 1 (69), pp. 274-282.

Forms of Verse Translation and the Translation of Verse Form

Literature, Roland Barthes has suggested, is of two classes. In the first place there is the class of poetry, fiction, and drama, in which a writer uses language to, as he says, "speak about objects and phenomena which, whether imaginary or not, are external and anterior to language." Besides this there is a class of writing which "deals not with 'the world', but with the linguistic formulations made by others; it is a comment on a comment."[1]

In defining this "secondary language or *meta*-language" (as he calls it), Barthes is concerned primarily with criticism, but the range of what I should prefer to designate meta-literature[2] is actually much broader. Round a poem, for instance, a wide variety of meta-literature can accumulate; some of the major forms might be indicated schematically as in the diagram on the next page.[3]

At the one edge of this fan of meta-literary forms is the form which primarily interests Barthes, critical comment on the poem written in the language of the poem. The practitioner of this first form, though he has to solve major interpretative problems if his results are to have validity, has in other words the advantage of being able to solve them within the same linguistic system on which the poem itself draws. The second form, the critical essay written in another language, shares with the first the fact that, as an essay, it is essentially indeterminate[4] in length, and also in subject matter: the critic can run on for as long as he cares to, and bring in whatever material he thinks relevant, to deal with even the shortest poem. At the same time this second form manifests a number of traits also characteristic of forms three and four: in a very real if special sense it "translates" the poem into another linguistic system as well as providing a critical interpretation of it. Form three, the prose translation, embraces a number of sub-forms, varying from the verbatim (interlinear, "literal", "word-for-word")[5] and the rank-bound[6] translation to the unbound "literary" translation attempting to transfer more elusive qualities of the original poem;[7] all these sub-forms, though, share the fact that (like forms one and two) they use prose as their medium and (like form four) are essentially determinate in length and subject matter.

Form four, the verse translation, is like all the previous forms

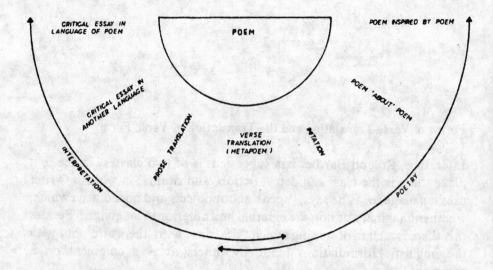

interpretative in intent, and like form three determinate in length and subject matter; at the same time it is fundamentally different from them, and like the remaining three forms, in the very basic fact that it makes use of verse as its medium, and hence manifestly aspires to be a poem in its own right, about which a new fan of meta-literature can take shape. Forms five, six, and seven, the imitation (in John Dryden's sense),[8] the poem drawing from the original in an indirect, partial way, and the poem only vaguely, generally inspired by the original, are like the verse translation and unlike the first three forms in their medium, but unlike forms three and four in the increasing indeterminacy of their length and subject matter, and unlike all the first four forms in the absence of interpretation of the original as one of their major purposes.

As this brief morphology re-emphasizes, all translation is an act of critical interpretation, but there are some translations of poetry which differ from all other interpretative forms in that they also have the aim of being acts of poetry — though it should immediately be pointed out that this poetry is of a very special kind, referring not to Barthes' "objects and phenomena... external and anterior to language", but to another linguistic object: the original poem. I have suggested elsewhere that amidst the general confusion in the terminology of translation studies it might be helpful if for this specific literary form, with its double purpose as meta-literature and as primary literature, we introduced the designation "metapoem".[9]

By virtue of its double purpose, the metapoem is a nexus of a complex bundle of relationships converging from two directions: from the original poem, in its language, and linked in a very specific way to the poetic tradition of that language; and from the poetic tradition of the target language, with its more or less stringent expectations regarding poetry which the metapoem, if it is to be successful as poetry, must in some measure meet.

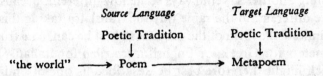

This complex series of relationships gives rise to various tensions that are absent, or at least less emphatically present, in other kinds of translations. One primary source of tension lies in the problem of choosing the most appropriate form of verse in which to cast the metapoem.[10]

What should the verse form of a metapoem be? There is, surely, no other problem of translation that has generated so much heat, and so little light, among the normative critics. Poetry, says one, should be translated into prose.[11] No, says a second, it should be translated into verse, for in prose its very essence is lost.[12] By all means into verse, and into the form of the original, argues a third.[13] Verse into verse, fair enough, says a fourth, but God save us from Homer in English hexameters.[14]

The attention of critics for this problem, if not their overconfidence in the universal validity of their own solutions to it, is understandable, for in the intricate process of decision-making which translation is,[15] the decision regarding the verse form to be used, made as it must be at a very early stage in the entire process, can be largely determinative for the nature and sequence of the decisions still to come, It is, then, perhaps worth our while to lay aside prescription in favour of description, and to survey systematically the various solutions that have been found.

Traditionally, translators have chosen between four approaches to the problem. (A fifth has been simply to sidestep it, by rendering the poem in prose. Technically, this might be considered as a kind of nil-form solution, but it would seem more satisfactory to keep to the classification proposed above, relegating the product of this approach to form three and concerning ourselves here only with form four, the translation which chooses to render poetry as poetry.)

The first traditional approach is that usually described as retaining the form of the original. Actually, since a verse form cannot exist outside language (though it is a convenient fiction that it can), it follows that no form can be "retained" by the translator as he moves from a source language to his target language. For this reason it is also preferable to avoid the term "identical form": no verse form in any one language can be entirely identical with a verse form in any other, however similar their nomenclatures and however cognate the languages. What in reality happens is that, much as one dancer may perform a pattern of steps closely resembling another's, yet always somehow different, because the two dancers are different, in the same way the translator taking this first approach will imitate the form of the original as best he can, constructing German hexameters for Greek, or English *terza rima* for Italian.[16] This approach, which might therefore best be described as one of "mimetic form", can be formulated as follows:

$$(1) \quad F_P \underset{.}{\sim} F_{MP} \qquad \qquad \text{(mimetic form)}$$

where F_P designates the verse form of the original poem, F_{MP} that of the metapoem, and $\underset{.}{\sim}$ fundamental similarity.

The translator making use of mimetic form looks squarely at the original poem when making his choice of verse form, to the exclusion of all other considerations.[17] A second school of translators has traditionally looked beyond the original poem itself to the function of its form within its poetic tradition, then sought a form that filled a parallel function within the poetic tradition of the target language. Since the *Iliad* and *Gerusalemme liberata* are epics, the argument of this school goes, an English translation should be in a verse form appropriate to the epic in English: blank verse or the heroic couplet. The principle underlying this approach is that of "analogical form", which might be formulated in this way:

$$(2) \quad F_P : PT_{SL} :: F_{MP} : PT_{TL} \qquad \qquad \text{(analogical form)}$$

where PT_{SL} indicates the poetic tradition of the source language, and PT_{TL} that of the target language.

Both the mimetic form and the analogical can be classified on a second plane as "form-derivative" forms, determined as they are by the principle of seeking some kind of equivalence in the target language for the outward form of the original poem. It is a relationship that can be formulated:

$$(1 \& 2) \quad (C_P \leftrightarrow F_P) \underset{TR}{\rightrightarrows} F_{MP} \rightarrow C_{MP} \qquad \text{(form-derivative forms)}$$

where C_P indicates the "content", the non-formal material, of the original poem, C_{MP} that of the metapoem, and $\underset{TR}{\rightarrow}$ the translingual process.

Today many translators have turned away from form-derivative form in favour of a third approach to the problem, resorting to a verse form which is basically "content-derivative", and might be called "organic form". The translator pursuing this approach does not take the form of the original as his starting point, fitting the content into a mimetic or analogical form as best he can, but starts from the semantic material, allowing it to take on its own unique poetic shape as the translation develops. This organic approach might be formulated as follows:

$$(3) \qquad (F_P \leftharpoonup C_P) \underset{TR}{\to} C_{MP} \to F_{MP} \qquad \text{(content-derivative form)}$$

Alongside these three major types of derivative form is a fourth type of form which has had its practitioners, if not its theoreticians, through the years. This form does not derive from the original poem at all, and might therefore be classified as "deviant form" or "extraneous form". The translator making use of this approach casts the metapoem into a form that is in no way implicit in either the form or the content of the original:

$$(4) \qquad (F_P \leftharpoonup C_P) \underset{TR}{\to} C_{MP} \leftharpoonup F_{MP} \qquad \text{(extraneous form)}$$

Each of these four types of metapoetic form, the mimetic, the analogical, the organic, and the extraneous, by its nature opens up certain possibilities for the translator who chooses it, and at the same time closes others. The effect of the analogical form is to bring the original poem within the native tradition, to "naturalize" it. Pope's *Iliad*, in rhymed couplets, becomes something very much like an English poem about English gentlemen, for all the Greek trappings of the fable. It follows that the analogical form is the choice to be expected in a period that is inturned and exclusive, believing that its own norms provide a valid touchstone by which to test the literature of other places and other times. Periods of this kind tend moreover to have such highly developed genre concepts that any type of form other than the analogical would be quite unacceptable to the prevailing literary taste. It is understandable, then, that the analogical form was the dominant metapoetic form during the neo-classical eighteenth century.[18]

The mimetic form, on the other hand, tends to have the effect of re-emphasizing, by its strangeness, the strangeness which for the target-language reader is inherent in the semantic message of the original poem. Rather than interpreting the original in terms of the native tradition, the mimetic metapoem requires the reader to stretch the limits of his literary sensibility, to extend his view beyond the bounds of what is recognized as acceptable in his own literary tradition. In some cases (as in the blank-verse translations of Shakespeare into German, or of the English Romantics into Dutch) the result may be a permanent enrichment of the target literary tradition with new formal resources. It follows that the mimetic form tends to come to the fore among translators in a period when genre concepts are weak, literary norms are being called into question, and the target culture as a whole stands open to outside impulses. Hence it is understandable that the mimetic form became the dominant metapoetic form during the nineteenth century.

The mimetic and the analogical form, as form-derivative forms, share the fact that they are the result of what is essentially a mechanical and dualistic approach to the basic nature of poetry: the poet chooses a form into which he then pours what he has to say, his ideas, thoughts, images, music, or whatever, and the metapoet follows suit. The organic form of the metapoem, on the other hand, is a corollary of an organic and monistic approach to poetry as a whole: since form and content are inseparable (are, in fact, one and the same thing within the reality of the poem), it is impossible to find any predetermined extrinsic form into which a poem can be poured in translation, and the only solution is to allow a new intrinsic form to develop from the inward workings of the text itself. As fundamentally pessimistic regarding the possibilities of cross-cultural transference as the mimetic approach is fundamentally optimistic, the organic approach has naturally come to the fore in the twentieth century.

There remains the extraneous form, which on closer examination is perhaps in some cases not so extraneous after all, but an older collateral of the organic form: a kind of minimum conformation on the part of the metapoet to the formal requirements of his poetic culture, which at the same time leaves him the freedom to transfer the "meaning" of the poem with greater flexibility than a mimetic or analogical form would have allowed. At any rate, the extraneous form has had a tenacious life as a kind of underground, minority form alongside the other possibilities ever since the seventeenth century. Rather than a period form, it has been a constant across the years, resorted to particularly by metapoets who lean in the direction of the imitation.

Yet the mimetic and analogical forms, too, must be viewed not solely as period forms, but also as literary constants which have continued to exert an influence long after their heyday. Henry Francis Cary translated the *Divine Comedy* in analogical blank verse in the dominantly mimetic nineteenth century, and many a translator has tried his hand at mimetic *terza rima* in the basically organic twentieth. In fact, the mimetic and analogical forms are still so much alive today that in recent years two distinguished contemporary translators have each given us English renderings of both the *Iliad* and the *Odyssey*, one, Richmond Lattimore, translating in hexameters, the other, Robert Fitzgerald, in blank verse. In the organic mode, on the other hand, our time has produced only two books of the *Iliad* by Christopher Logue and the passages from the *Odyssey* in Ezra Pound's *Cantos*.

Quotations from three of these contemporary translations may serve to illustrate some of the forms I have attempted to define in this essay. The passage I should like to cite is from the *Odyssey*, the opening lines of Book XI, which describe the departure of Ulysses and his men from the island of Circe. The first version is in Fitzgerald's analogical blank verse:

We bore down on the ship at the sea's edge
and launched her on the salt immortal sea,
stepping our mast and spar in the black ship;
embarked the ram and ewe and went aboard
in tears, with bitter and sore dread upon us.
But now a breeze came up for us astern —
a canvas-bellying landbreeze, hale shipmate
sent by the singing nymph with sun-bright hair;
so we made fast the braces, took our thwarts,
and let the wind and steersman work the ship
with full sail spread all day above our coursing,
till the sun dipped, and all the ways grew dark
upon the fathomless unresting sea.
                          By night
our ship ran onward toward the Ocean's bourne,
the realm and region of the Men of Winter,
hidden in mist and cloud. Never the flaming
eye of Helios lights on those men
at morning, when he climbs the sky of stars,
nor in descending earthward out of heaven;
ruinous night being rove over those wretches.[19]

The second version, by Lattimore, is in mimetic hexameters:

Now when we had gone down again to the sea and our vessel,
first of all we dragged the ship down into the bright water,
and in the black hull set the mast in place, and set sails,
and took the sheep and walked them aboard, and ourselves also
embarked, but sorrowful, and weeping big tears. Circe
of the lovely hair, the dread goddess who talks with mortals,
sent us an excellent companion, a following wind, filling
the sails, to carry from astern the ship with the dark prow.
We ourselves, over all the ship making fast the running gear,
sat still, and let the wind and the steersman hold her steady.
All day long her sails were filled as she went through the water,
and the sun set, and all the journeying-ways were darkened.

She made the limit, which is of the deep-running Ocean.
There lie the community and city of Kimmerian people,
hidden in fog and cloud, nor does Helios, the radiant
sun, ever break through the dark, to illuminate them with his shining,
neither when he climbs up into the starry heaven,
nor when he wheels to return again from heaven to earth,
but always a glum night is spread over wretched mortals.[20]

In Pound's organic verse the same passage runs as follows:

And then went down to the ship,
Set keel to breakers, forth on the godly sea, and
We set up mast and sail on that swart ship,
Bore sheep aboard her, and our bodies also
Heavy with weeping, so winds from sternward
Bore us out onward with bellying canvas,
Circe's this craft, the trim-coifed goddess.
Then we sat amidships, wind jamming the tiller,
Thus with stretched sail, we went over sea till day's end.
Sun to his slumber, shadows o'er all the ocean,
Came we then to the bounds of deepest water,
To the Kimmerian lands, and peopled cities
Covered with close-webbed mist, unpiercèd ever
With glitter of sun-rays
Nor with stars stretched, nor looking back from heaven
Swartest night stretched over wretched men there.[21]

As these three quotations emphasize, there is an extremely close relationship between the kind of verse form a translator chooses and the kind of total effect his translation achieves. It is, in fact, a relationship so central to the entire problem of verse translation that its study deserves our utmost attention — study, not in order to arrive at normative dicta: So it must be, and not otherwise; but to come to understand the nature of various kinds of metapoem, each of which can never be more than a single interpretation out of many of the original whose image it darkly mirrors.

Notes

1. Roland Barthes, "Criticism as Language", in *The Critical Moment: Essays on the Nature of Literature* (London: Faber, 1964), pp. 123-129, quotation p. 126. Cf. René Wellek's similar remark regarding criticism: "Its aim is intellectual cognition. It does not create a fictional imaginative world such as the world of music or poetry." (René Wellek, "Literary Theory, Criticism, and History", in his *Concepts of Criticism* [New Haven: Yale University Press, 1963], pp. 1-20, quotation p. 4).
2. In order to avoid confusion with other, more common meanings given to the term "meta-language" in contemporary linguistics and philosophy.
3. These forms, of course, constitute only a segment from a larger arc which also includes the paraphrase and other derivative forms in the original language.
4. In the mathematical sense of determinacy: a work of meta-literature is

indeterminate in length and/or subject matter when its length and/or subject matter are not restricted by the length and/or subject matter of the work of original literature which occasions it, and is determinate when it is so restricted.

5. The term "literal translation" has a long lineage, but is less accurate than might be required of a technical expression: even the closest translation does not usually follow the original at a rank lower than the word. "Word-for-word translation", a term with an even longer lineage (deriving as it does from Cicero), is a more accurate, but also more awkward, designation for the same thing. Would "verbatim translation" or "lexical translation" not be more satisfactory terms than either of these two?

6. On the term rank-bound translation, see John C. Catford, *A Linguistic Theory of Translation: An Essay in Applied Linguistics* (London: Oxford University Press, 1965; Language and Language Learning, 8), esp. pp. 24-25; the term derives from the grammatical system proposed by M.A.K. Halliday in his "Categories of the Theory of Grammar", *Word* (New York), 17 (1961), 241-292. For an interesting application of the technique of rank-bound translation in the analysis of poetry translation, see Jean Ure, Alexander Rodger, and Jeffrey Ellis, "Somn: Sleep — An Exercise in the Use of Descriptive Linguistic Techniques in Literary Translation", *Babel* (Avignon), 15 (1969), 4-14, 73-82.

7. The commentary, paraphrase, and gloss in a second language should perhaps be included as transitional phases between forms two and three.

8. In his well-known tripartite classification: "All translation, I suppose, may be reduced to these three heads. First, that of metaphrase, or turning an author word by word, and line by line, from one language to another... The second is that of paraphrase, or translation with latitude, where the author is kept in view by the translator, so as never to be lost, but his words are not so strictly followed as his sense... The third way is that of imitation, where the translator (if now he has not lost that name) assumes the liberty not only to vary from the words and sense, but to forsake them both as he sees occasion; and taking only some general hints from the original, to run division on the ground-work, as he pleases." (John Dryden, "Preface to *Ovid's Epistles Translated by Several Hands* [1680]", in his *Of Dramatic Poesy and Other Critical Essays*, ed. George Watson [2 vols., London: Dent, 1962; Everyman's Library], I, 262-273, quotation p. 268).

9. See above, pp. 9-22, which paper also touches on a number of other points raised in the first part of this essay. Here, as there, I should point out that the term "metapoem" was previously used by John MacFarlane in a somewhat different sense, more or less synonymous with Dryden's imitation: see MacFarlane's "Modes of Translation", *Durham University Journal*, 45 (1952-1953), 77-93, esp. p. 90.

10. In what follows I use the word "form" in the most traditional and restricted sense, not to refer to the entire essential structure of the poem, its inward, organic, or "deep" form, but to describe only the surface framework within which this "deep" form takes shape: the outward or mechanical form of rhyme, metre (and/or rhythm), verse length, stanzaic patterning and division, and the like. The distinction is one much contested by contemporary literary critics, but nevertheless of quite some value to the analyst of the problem of verse translation.

11. See e.g. John Middleton Murry's adamant "Poetry ought always to be rendered into prose." Murry's argument is that "Since the aim of the translator should be to present the original as exactly as possible, no fetters of rhyme or metre should be imposed to hamper this difficult labour. Indeed they make it impossible." (Murry, "Classical Translations", in his *Pencillings: Little Essays on Literature* [London:

Collins, 1923], pp. 128-137, quotations p. 129).

12. See e.g. Alexander Fraser Tytler, who in his *Essay on the Principles of Translation* (London: Dent, n.d. [first published 1791]; Everyman's Library), formulated one of the chief arguments against the prose rendering: "To attempt a translation of a lyric poem into prose, is the most absurd of all undertakings; for those very characters of the original which are essential to it, and which constitute its highest beauties, if transferred to a prose translation, become unpardonable blemishes." (p. 111).

13. Perhaps the ablest defence of this point of view in English, in theory if not in practice, was that of Matthew Arnold, who demanded a Homer in English hexameters — though he immediately proceeded to point out that they must be "good English hexameters": see his series of lectures *On Translating Homer* (London: Longman, 1861). In other languages, if not in English, this point of view is today still frequently advocated as the only possible one; see e.g. the remark (in connection with the work of one of the translators for the Russian English-language review *Soviet Literature*) that "Like most of our other translators of poetry she considers it essential to convey in English the rhythm and rhyme pattern of the original. The tradition of rhymed metric verse is fully alive in modern Soviet poetry and even though free and blank verse may be predominant in the West we feel it would be wrong to make Soviet poets fit an alien standard." (Valentina Jacque, "Our Translators", *Soviet Literature* [Moscow], 1968, No. 6, pp. 175-180, quotation p. 178).

14. The attitude of almost every critic over the past hundred years to touch on the controversy between Arnold and Francis William Newman (see Arnold's lectures mentioned in note 13 and Newman's *Homeric Translation in Theory and Practice* [London & Edinburgh: Williams and Norgate, 1861]) has been to despair of creating a hexameter capable of serving as a feasible English metre for Homer. Only the recent translations of Richmond Lattimore have brought a change in this attitude.

15. Cf. the last article by Jiří Levý, his "Translation as a Decision Process", in *To Honor Roman Jakobson: Essays on the Occasion of His Seventieth Birthday, 11 October 1966* (3 vols., The Hague: Mouton, 1967), II, 1171-1182.

16. The analogue of dancing is borrowed from W. Haas, who uses it to describe the transfer of meaning in the process of translation as a whole: see his "The Theory of Translation", in George H.R. Parkinson (ed.), *The Theory of Meaning* (London: Oxford University Press, 1968), pp. 86-108, reference p. 104. Haas' study was originally published as an article in *Philosophy* (London), 37 (1962), 208-228.

17. There is also a kind of "pseudo-mimetic" or "mock-mimetic" approach in which the translator looks more at the names of forms than at the forms themselves. Various translators, for instance, have felt called upon to translate the French Classical playwrights into English alexandrines, guided (or misguided) by the belief that they were in some way "equivalent" to French alexandrines, which in fact they are not, either in form or in function. This pseudo-mimetic form is only one of a number of sub-forms, mixed forms, and variants that have been neglected here in favour of a series of major categories which are at best Weberian ideal-types and cannot be considered to do full justice to the wide diversity of actual pratice.

18. Here and in the following remarks I have based my observations primarily on the literary history of translation in the Western European languages (though even there the French, with their predilection for translations into prose, are something of an exception); I am not sure that what I have to say applies with equal force to the Slavic literatures. Outside the European tradition, of course, it would not seem to apply at all. In the translation of non-European verse into European languages,

incidentally, the additional problems have always served to reduce the ranks of the mimeticists; to understand why, one has only to think of the issues involved in translating the semantic content of, say, a Chinese poem within the strict confines of a mimetic form.

19. *The Odyssey*, tr. Robert Fitzgerald (Garden City, N.Y.: Doubleday, 1961), Book XI, ll. 1-20.

20. *The Odyssey*, tr. Richmond Lattimore (New York, Evanston, and London: Harper, 1967), Book XI, ll. 1-19.

21. Ezra Pound, *Seventy Cantos* (London: Faber & Faber, 1950), Canto I, ll. 1-16 (first published in book form in *A Draft of XVI Cantos* [Paris: Three mountain press, 1925]). Some of the semantic differences in Pound's version are a result of the fact that he relied heavily on Andreas Divus' humanist translation (1538) into Latin: on Divus see Pound's essay "Translators of Greek: Early Translators of Homer", in his *Literary Essays* (T.S. Eliot ed.; London: Faber & Faber,, 1954), pp. 249-275, esp. pp. 259-267 (the section on Divus was first published in 1918).

"The Cross-Temporal Factor in Verse Translation" is the revised text of a paper presented at Nitra, Slovakia, in September 1969. First published in *Slavica Slovaca* (Bratislava), 6 (1971), pp. 326-334, and reprinted in *Meta* (Montreal), 17 (1972), pp. 102-110.

The Cross-Temporal Factor in Verse Translation

Writers on translation (translation, that is to say, in the sense which Roman Jakobson has termed "interlingual translation"[1]) have usually tended to neglect the "cross-temporal"[2] factor in the process, abstracting it instead as a synchronic process in order to concentrate on problems that are no doubt more central. There is, however, a set of problems specific to translating a text that not only was written in another language but derives from another time, and it is perhaps worth our while to take a closer look at these problems of cross-temporal translation.

The formal model of translation as a communication process is well known. In simplified terms it is this. A person who can be called the source (S) encodes a message (M) in a specific language (A) and transmits it to a receiver (R_A). This receiver, as translator, then performs a kind of "translingual transfer" ($\underset{TR}{=} >$) to encode in a second language (B) a new message (M_B) that is intended to "mean the same as" or "correspond to" or "be equivalent to" the original message, or at any rate to give the illusion of doing some of these things.[3] Functioning as a new source (S_B), the translator then transmits this new message to a new receiver (R_B).

$$(1) \quad S_A \rightarrow M_A \rightarrow R_A \underset{TR}{=} > S_B \rightarrow M_B \rightarrow R_B$$

For many aspects of translation theory it is convenient to simplify this model to the formulation

$$(2) \quad M_A \underset{TR}{=} \rightarrow M_B$$

or, introducing the inelegant but standard terms "source language" (SL) and "target language" (TL), to

$$(3) \quad M_{SL} \underset{TR}{=} \rightarrow M_{TL}$$

In the case of verse translation the simplified model can be stated in terms of poem (P) and "metapoem"[4] (MP)

$$(4) \quad P_{SL} \underset{TR}{=} \rightarrow MP_{TL}$$

Obviously in this last case, which might be termed the model of the "metapoetic process", much more is in reality involved in the transfer $\underset{TR}{=}$>than purely a shift from one linguistic system to another. Simultaneously there is a shift from what may be called, in the largest sense, the socio-cultural system within which the poet operated to the socio-cultural system of the metapoet; and on a more restricted level there is a shift from the literary or poetic system[5] within which the poem has its place to the literary sytem in terms of which the metapoem must find expression. On each of these three levels, the general level of the socio-cultural system and the more specific levels of the linguistic and literary systems, the translator is faced by inter-system incompatibilities that he must resolve, or in any case deal with in such a way as to give the reader of the metapoem the illusion they have been resolved.

When the poem to be translated is a contemporary one, the translator can approach each of these pairs of systems synchronically, as if they were static systems, frozen in time. Actually, of course, they are in constant change, and the translator of a poem of another age cannot ignore this fact, which confronts him with a series of problems in which the cross-temporal factor may loom as large as the interlingual. Moreover it would appear that translators tend to deal with these cross-temporal problems in ways that are quite similar to the approaches of native speakers who are reading a non-contemporary poem. If this is true, the translator's solutions would seem to have a relevance beyond the field of translation studies alone.

Let me turn to an example. There is a rondel by Charles d'Orléans that runs like this:

Jeunes amoureux nouveaulx,
En la nouvelle saison,
Par les rues, sans raison,
Chevauchent faisans les saulx.

Et font sailler des carreaulx
Le feu, comme de charbon:
Jeunes amoureux nouveaulx
En la nouvelle saison.

Je ne sçay si leurs travaulx
Ilz employent bien ou non;
Mais piqués de l'esperon
Sont autant que leurs chevaulx,
Jeunes amoureux nouveaulx.[6]

Now clearly, for all the apparent simplicity of this poem, it is a highly intricate structure containing features that would not have been easy for a fifteenth-century contemporary of Charles d'Orléans (or for that matter the Duke himself)[7] to render into English. These features are not our direct concern here, but I would call attention to the syllabic verse system (as opposed to the English accentual or accentual-syllabic); the sustained rhyme and the complex rondel form; the contrapuntal use of the word *nouveaulx/nouvelle*, occurring five times in all, and lending emphasis to the major theme of the poem; the general absence of adjectives other than *nouveaulx/nouvelle* (and the supporting *jeunes* — three occurrences), which serves to foreground[8] these two words even more; the delay in complete explicitation of the major imagic element *chevaulx* until the penultimate line; and the shift from objective to subjective and from descriptive to commentative in the last stanza.

The translator of today, unlike his counterpart of the fifteenth century, cannot consider these features by themselves; he must relate them to a series of cross-temporal problems. These problems, too, are not solely linguistic, but also literary and socio-cultural. On the linguistic level, the translator must find a solution for the fact that the poem is written in an older *état de langue* or "temporal dialect"[9]: should he reflect this in some way in his translation, and if so, how? On the literary or poetic level he must for instance consider what is to be done with the rondel form — in Charles d'Orléans' time a lively, much-used verse form, and actually one of the least complex of the forms of the day; now a relic of a bygone poetic tradition felt to be more appropriate for a *jeu d'esprit* than for serious verse. And on the socio-cultural level the translator must face up to the fact that the central image of the poem, young men riding on horseback to impress the girls, has lost its compelling force: their counterparts today ride motor-bikes or drive cars. (Similarly the subsidiary metaphor of sparks from charcoal, then a reference to a familiar, everyday event, is now a "literary" reference remote from life.)

In all such instances, and on each of the various levels, the translator must make a choice. The choice in each individual case may be to attempt to retain the specific aspect of the original poem, even though that aspect is now experienced as historical rather than as directly relevant today; this approach might be called "historicizing translation" or "retentive translation". Or the choice may be to seek "equivalents" (which are, of course, always equivalent only to a greater or lesser degree) to "re-create" a contemporary relevance, an approach that could be called "modernizing translation" or "re-creative translation."[10]

Actually, this bipolar model of "historicizing" (H) *versus* "modernizing" (M) or "retentive" *versus* "re-creative" is rather more stylized than reality. On the linguistic level, for instance, there is not solely a choice between translating Charles d'Orléans' poem into fifteenth-century English or the English of today. Theoretically, in fact, there is a whole range of possible choices. For practical purposes, though, the target literary system dictates one of three[11]: (1) The poem is rendered in a replica of fifteenth-century English; (2) The poem is rendered in a variety of what Geoffrey Leech has called "standard archaic usage",[12] the poetic idiom created round the time of Shakespeare and Spenser and used with greater or lesser modifications till early in the present century; (3) The poem is rendered in a modern poetic idiom, an idiom that might be characterized by its willingness to integrate almost any linguistic material *but* standard archaic usage.[13] (This third idiom must in turn be divided into two sub-varieties, "early" or "traditional" modern and "experimental modern" or "contemporary", both of which are acceptable to large groups of poetry reader today.[14]) The first of these three choices, rendering in the language of the author's day, might be labelled H, while later non-modern choices might be indicated as H_1, H_2, H_3... H_n, and the choice of modern idiom M (with a sub-distinction M_1 for "traditional modern" and M_2 for "contemporary").

With these remarks in mind, it is worth our while to look briefly at four recent translations of the rondel *Jeunes amoureux nouveaulx*. All these translations are contemporary: they were, in fact, all published for the first time only a few years ago. None of them is by a poet or translator of renown (actually they are the winning submissions in a "weekend competition" set by the *New Statesman* in March 1969),[15] but they serve to illustrate some of the points I am attempting to make.

The first of the versions, by Adam Khan, is clearly historicizing in its overall approach. The language presents itself as medieval (out of 55 lexical items there are 32, constituting 25 different words, that are identifiable as belonging to the temporal dialect of Middle English), and more particularly as the language of the anonymous lyrics of the English fourteenth and fifteenth centuries. Prosodically, the translation is "mimetic" in preserving the rondel form, "historicizing analogical"[16] in substituting accentual verse with a varying number of syllables and feet (the verse pattern of the anonymous lyrics) for the syllabic verse of the French, with its strict adherence to seven syllables per line. (In Charles d'Orléans' own translations of rondels into English he preferred a quite regular accentual-syllabic line of ten syllables, a more courtly, less popular verse form.) As might be expected in a translation that is historicizing in both its linguistic and its literary approach, the socio-cultural situation of the original has been retained as well.

> Lusty yonge bacheleres,
> In the Spring sesoun,
> Ryden the stretes sans resoun,
> Making to-lepen hir coursers.

And strykken al-over
Fyr fro everich stoon:
Lusty yonge bacheleres
In the Spring sesoun.

I noot nat yif hir labours
Been to gode or il chosen;
But prikke of spore felen
Even as doon hir coursers,
Lusty yonge bacheleres.

If the general approach of a translator to the cross-temporal factors (D) involved in a translation can be considered as a set, and if his approach to the cross-temporal aspects of the linguistic (1), literary or poetic (p), and socio-cultural (s) systems reflected in the poem can be posited as the three items in that set

(5) D (1,p,s)

then the approach of this translator must be qualified as (H,H,H). Mr. Khan's metapoem, like the original, comes to the present-day English reader through the haze of history, and it confronts the reader in English with much the same kinds of interpretative problems as does one of Charles d'Orléans' own English poems.

In the translation by Gavin Ewart the emphasis is quite different. The horse-riding theme is retained, and as a result there is little in the lexical items taken individually to mark them as specifically of the twentieth century, but nevertheless the general effect of the poem is decidedly contemporary. This is to a large degree the result of formal decisions. The amphibrachic metre and the exclusively feminine rhymes, both of them unusual in English, in conjunction lend a drive to the verse that underscores the poem's theme in an unusual fashion. The variation of the two opening lines in lines seven and eight (instead of the full repetition required by the rondel form) serves to foreground the form of the original by means of what Jiří Levý has termed "anti-style"[17] — a technique which is quite probably one of the distinguishing features of contemporary poetry. This translator's approach can be qualified as (M_2,M_2,H).

Young lovers beginning
begin a new season,
fill streets with unreason,
ride around, spinning,

bright sparks on paving
like fires in the autumn:
young lovers behaving
like mares in their season.

I don't know if they're sinning
against Time, or erring;
but under Love's spurring
they're horses — and winning,
young lovers beginning.

A translation by Peter Rowlett is, aside from one feature, demonstrative of an approach to cross-temporal translation that is more usual than either Mr. Ewart's or Mr. Khan's. Retaining the socio-cultural situation of the original, Mr. Rowlett has written an English "metapoem" that is "traditional modern" in lexis and syntax, and prosodically in a form that is compatible with either traditional-modern or standard archaic usage. (The one exceptional feature lies in the word "prick", which is introduced as synonymous with "spur", but in the context very clearly has the meaning of "penis" as well. In the second sense out of place in a poetic text in any idiom except the contemporary, the word is introduced here with singular effect to organize and explicitize the central metaphor of the poem, but at the same time it lends an ironic dimension to the traditional-modern idiom and traditional form that in a way resembles the tension between courtly form and meditative content that has been detected in Charles d'Orléans' own later verse.) Mr. Rowlett's approach might be qualified as $(M_{1(2)}, M_1/H, H)$.[18]

Hot young lovers, season-sick,
Bruning with the year's advance
Roam the restless streets of France;
As their stallions wheel and kick

The flinty cobbles sharp and quick
The sparks fly like a fiery lance.
Hot young lovers, season-sick,
Burning with the year's advance.

God knows what makes the youngsters tick
Or even if they like the dance ...
The spur's what makes the stallion prance:
They too are governed by the prick.
Hot young lovers, season-sick.

Another translation, by G.R. Nicholson, contains one major feature that distinguishes it strikingly from the others. This is the contemporization of the socio-cultural system, that is to say, the updating of the theme from horseback-riding swains to motorcycle-riding "rockers". Paralleling this feature is a contemporization of lexis: five different words (ten lexical items) date from within the past twenty years in the sense in which they are used in the metapoem, and several others are typically twentieth-century. The verse form, by contrast, is at best traditional-modern, and so functionally is in marked irony to the "with-it" tone of the idiom. The approach in this version might be qualified as $(M_2, M_1/H, M)$.[19]

> Young rockers with a bird in tow,
> Now the long evenings are here,
> Reviving their engines, changing gear,
> Up and down the streets they go.
>
> They do a ton-up, just for show
> Along a stretch not far from here:
> Young rockers with a bird in tow,
> Now the long evenings are here.
>
> Whether they're having it or no
> I'm left to wonder, but it's clear
> The engine's music in their ear
> Speaks for the urge that works them so,
> Young rockers with a bird in tow.

Put in the form of a table, the approaches of the four translators can be classified as follows:

| Translator | Linguistic | Literary[1] | | Socio-Cultural |
		Verse (General)	Rondel Form	
		System		
Khan	H	H	H	H
Ewart	M_2	M_2	M_2	H
Rowlett	$M_{1(2)}$	M_1	H	H
Nicholson	M_2	M_1	H	M

[1] Here broken down into the two sub-aspects introduced above: see n. 18.

Two things strike the eye in this table. First there is the fact that of the four translations only Mr. Khan's is of one piece, the others combining a historicizing approach at one level with a modernizing at another, and none of them modernized at all levels. A cursory examination of other translations of older poetry into and from various languages led to findings which support this analysis. There would seem to be particular resistance to transposing a poem of another day into a metapoem that is completely modern on all levels, with nothing in it to indicate its ties with an earlier time. If this hypothesis is correct, it means that the inclination to classify translations as modernizing or historicizing from an overall point of view must be abandoned in favour of a more elaborate analysis establishing a more complex profile for each translation.

It may very well be that once that is done on a larger scale, and in more detail than it has been possible to do here, we shall also discover that the pressures towards (and the resistance to) either modernizing or historicizing are different in regard to each of the various systems. This leads me to a second point to be detected from the table. If one is to judge from these four translations, there would seem to be particular resistance to modernizing in the socio-cultural sphere. Can it be said that the possibilities for re-creation rather than retention are more restricted in this sphere than in the linguistic and the literary, whereas in the other two spheres the pressures against retentive historicizing are greater? And have these possibilities and pressures varied from age to age and from country to country?

These are questions that come to the fore as a result of this preliminary study, but for anything more than a highly provisional answer to them a more complex analytical method needs to be developed. In developing that method the translation analyst will have to rely first and foremost on the techniques and findings of contemporary literary and linguistic research. But at the same time he will have to evolve his own terms and techniques, adapted to the problems specific to his field of study. This paper is intended as a step in that direction.

Notes

1. Roman Jakobson, "On Linguistic Aspects of Translation", in *On Translation*, ed. Reuben A. Brower, Cambridge (Mass.): Harvard University Press, 1959, pp. 232-239, see p. 233.

2. I have preferred the term "cross-temporal" to "diachronic" for two reasons: (1) "diachronic" has come to be used primarily in regard to languages to the exclusion of other systems viewed in a temporal perspective, and (2) even within the linguistic context it tends to refer to developments over a range in time rather than the kind of contrastive study of two *états de langue* that is involved in the cross-temporal translation process.

3. That the new message should "mean the same" as the original message is, of course, the popular conception; that it should "correspond to" or "be equivalent to" it is the point of view advanced by Eugene A. Nida, J.C. Catford, and other prominent theorists of translation. The creating of an "illusion" of equivalence is, I should suggest, a factor of greater importance, at least in literary translation, than has usually been recognized. On this point see also Jiří Levý, *Die literarische Übersetzung: Theorie einer Kunstgattung*, Frankfurt am Main & Bonn: Athenäum Verlag, "Athenäum Bücher zur Dichtkunst", 1969, pp. 31-32.

4. For the term "metapoem" see pp. 9-22 and 23-33 above.

5. I use this term to indicate the entire system of literary and (more specifically) poetic conventions within which (or in revolt against which) a poem is written. In this brief paper it has been convenient to focus attention on such surface patterns as rhythm, metre, and rhyme and their function within the poetic system, but the term is intended to include more complex patterns and relationships as well.

6. The text is cited here as it was given in the *New Statesman* competition (see below, n. 15). The standard text (to be found in Charles d'Orléans, *Poésies*, ed. Pierre Champion, 2 vols., Paris, Librairie ancienne Honoré Champion, 1923 and 1927, I, 247), has the following textual differences: ll. 1, 7, 13 *read* Jennes *for* Jeunes; 1. 6 *read* cherbon *for* charbon; 1. 10 *read* emploient *for* employent. In ll. 7, 8, and 13 square brackets are used to indicate the words not written out in the manuscript but obviously meant to be repeated. Three valuable recent studies to deal at length with the fifteenth-century poet and his verse are Norma L. Goodrich, *Charles of Orleans: A Study of Themes in His French and in His English Poetry*, Geneva: Droz, 1967; Daniel Poirion, *Le Lexique de Charles d'Orléans dans les ballades*, Geneva: Droz, 1967; and John Fox, *The Lyric Poetry of Charles d'Orléans*, Oxford: Clarendon Press, 1969.

7. The texts of Charles' poems in English, written during the quarter century of imprisonment after his capture at Agincourt, were edited by Robert Steele for the Early English Text Society (vols. 215 and 220) as *The English Poems of Charles d'Orléans*, 2 vols., London: Oxford University Press, 1941 and 1946. For a discussion of the English verse, see the book by Goodrich referred to in n. 6.

8. The term introduced by Paul L. Garvin as a translation of the Czech *aktualisace*. See his *A Prague School Reader on Esthetics, Literary Structure, and Style*, Washington (D.C.): Washington Linguistic Club, 1958.

9. The term used e.g. by John C. Catford: see his *A Linguistic Theory of Translation: An Essay in Applied Linguistics* (London: Oxford University Press, "Language and Language Learning, 8", 1965), pp. 88-89.

10. The two terms "retentive translation" and "re-creative translation", unlike the other pair, have a broader relevance than in the cross-temporal situation alone, and might be roughly equated with Eugene A. Nida's "formal-equivalence translation" and "dynamic-equivalence translation": see his *Toward a Science of Translating, with Special Reference to Principles and Procedures Involved in Bible Translating*, Leiden: Brill, 1964, pp. 159-160, 165-177. The term "modernizing translation" has an ancestor in the concept of "modernization" or "Anglicizing" applied in the seventeenth and eighteenth centuries to English translations of the classics.

11. Or, for certain specific purposes (to achieve irony, for instance), a combination of them.

12. Geoffrey N. Leech, *A Linguistic Guide to English Poetry*, London: Longmans, "English Language Series", 1969, p. 13. Leech bases his definition of this style on the detailed studies of Bernard Groom, *The Diction of Poetry from Spenser to Bridges*, Toronto: Toronto University Press, 1955.

13. Except when that can be used for facetious or ironic purposes.

14. Though there are indications that the "early modern" idiom is being experienced by a growing number of readers of poetry as historical.

15. Competition No. 2,039, set by Ann Arbor, results reported in the *New Statesman* for 11 April 1969.

16. On the terms "mimetic" and "analogical" see p. 26 above.

17. In his "Mathematical Aspects of the Theory of Verse", in Lubomír Doležel and Richard W. Bailey (eds.), *Statistics and Style* (New York: American Elsevier, 1969,

"Mathematical Linguistics and Automatic Language Processing, 6"), pp. 95-112.

18. In the case of this and the next translation it seemed appropriate to break down the approach to the literary systems into two sub-aspects: the approach to the general problem of verse form (here qualified M_1) and the approach to the more specific problem of what to do with the rondel form as such (here H). Inclusion of other more complex aspects of the literary system in the analysis would no doubt lead to a more clearly delineated profile of the translator's approach than it has been possible to define here.

19. Form and idiom support each other more harmoniously in another rendering by Mr. Nicholson, in which a verse system very similar to that in the translation quoted above is fused with a lexis and syntax that border on the standard archaic:

Young lovers with new love aglow,
In the springtime of the year,
Through the streets in wild career
On their prancing horses go.

Their horseshoes from the flagstones throw,
Fire that like sparks from coals appear:
Young lovers with new love aglow
In the springtime of the year.

What profit their love's labours show
I know not, not what loss they bear;
Under the spur their horses rear
But they a spur more mordant know,
Young lovers with new love aglow.

The two translations were submitted to the *New Statesman* as a pair, and I am probably doing Mr. Nicholson less than justice by dealing with one of them in isolation.

"Rebuilding the Bridge at Bommel: Notes on the Limits of Translatability" is a slightly revised version of a paper presented to the Netherlandic Section of the Modern Language Association at the annual convention held in Chicago, 27-30 December 1971. First published in *DQR: Dutch Quarterly Review of Anglo-American Letters* (Assen), 2 (1972), pp. 65-72 and reprinted in *Modern Poetry in Translation* (London), No. 26 (Autumn 1976), pp. 20-23. A Dutch translation was published under the title "De brug bij Bommel herbouwen" in the review *De Revisor* (Amsterdam), 3 (1976), No. 5, pp. 36-39. A Slovak version appeared in *Slavica Slovaca* (Bratislava), 8 (1973), pp. 399-404.

Rebuilding the Bridge at Bommel: Notes on the Limits of Translatability

Is poetry translatable? It is a question that has been argued long and furiously, but the debates have usually generated more heat than light. At one extreme are those who consider that every text, hence all poetry, can be transferred from one language to another without substantial loss. Let us call them the radical left. At the opposite extreme are those who contend that no text in one language is ever completely equivalent to any text in another language, and consequently that all translation is impossible. Let us call *them* the radical right. In translation as in politics, most people take their stance in between the two extremes, believing that translation, of poetry at any rate, is sometimes possible, sometimes impossible; sometimes easy, sometimes difficult; sometimes a failure, sometimes an amazing success. A major argument in favour of this intermediate position is the fact that there does exist a wide range of verse translations, bad, indifferent, and good.

In contrast to the widespread willingness to pronounce opinions on the general question of whether or not poetry is translatable, serious attempts to define the specific problems of verse translation, and the specific limits imposing themselves, are all too few. Yet surely this is a much more fruitful field for discussion and research. Consider for instance a poem by Martinus Nijhoff, his sonnet "De moeder de vrouw", and more particularly the first line. I have chosen this line to examine further because, though its interpretation seems quite clear, its translation is a problem that has bothered me for years. The line runs: "Ik ging naar Bommel om de brug te zien".

What should the translator do with this line? Should he render it lexically (that is to say, word-for-word, what is usually but erroneously called "literally"): "I went to Bommel for the bridge to see"? Such a translation reflects the syntax of the Dutch, but is hardly English, let alone poetry. Or should he translate into a syntax that, in relation to the possibilities of English, seems to "match" or "be equivalent to" the syntax of the original in relation to the possibilities of Dutch: "I went to Bommel to see the bridge"? Yet that line, for all its matching syntax, has a rhythm in English reminiscent of a nursery rhyme more than anything else ("I went to London to visit the queen"), while the Dutch is the iambic opening line of a sonnet. Should the translator go a step further, adjusting his text to accommodate the sonnet metre of the line: "I went to Bommel for to see the bridge", "I went to Bommel to behold the bridge", "I went to Bommel, went to see the bridge"? Such an adjustment would make it possible for him to set an iambic pattern for the entire poem, and so to translate it in a sonnet form. Yet the adjustment can be made only at the price of a tonal shift from the near-colloquial to a more sedate and (at least in the case of the first two versions) archaizing and "poetic" style alien to the original line. At the same time the adjustment confronts the translator with a new problem: is he to reflect in some way the rhyme of the original as well as the metre, for instance by retaining the "Italian" sonnet form, or by substituting the "matching" English form (and the same time giving himself greater leeway)? If so, the word "bridge" at the end of the line has introduced a restriction on the degree of his translation freedom for at least one line further on, just as his choice of iambic metre constitutes a major restriction on his lexical and syntactic freedom throughout the rest of the poem.

There are still more problems. What, for instance, should the translator do with the place-name Bommel? For the Dutch reader the reference is perfectly clear, and can be fitted into a whole array of associations: "Zaltbommel kent u allemaal", "You all know Zaltbommel", says Van Egeraat in a standard Dutch guidebook. Indeed, the older Dutch reader, when he goes on to the next line ("Ik zag de nieuwe brug"), will even be able to date the poem to a time soon after that day in 1933 when a new bridge was opened across the River Waal at "Bommel", to the accompaniment of much publicity in the press. All this, of course, is lost on the English-language reader, who does not even know that Bommel is a place-name, so cannot search for it in the gazetteer, and would not find it if he did, since the official name of the town is not Bommel but Zaltbommel.

The translator can face up to this problem in various ways. He may retain the place, and do his best to clarify it in an explanatory note, which he can hope will provide enough information for the reader to feel at least vicariously involved. Or he may decide that Bommel and its bridge, as part of the *sujet* or discourse of the poem rather than its *fable* or story, can be replaced by a "matching" or "equivalent" object within the range of the reader's culture. A new bridge across an American river, for instance.

Yet that, too, broaches a new problem. Should this "new bridge" be sought in the American early thirties, so that the translation is fitted into the same temporal slot in literary and cultural history as the original? Or should the translator take advantage of the opportunity inherent in the act of translating a non-contemporary text, the opportunity to "foreground" the situation, hunting out a bridge built in our own day?

This has been a fairly exhaustive catalogue of the problems presenting themselves to the translator as he sets out to tackle this single line of seemingly simple verse. Some of the problems are local, restricted to this one line alone; others are general — that is, the solutions chosen for this first line will delimit the range of choices open to the translator in finding solutions to other problems arising later in the poem. None of the problems would seem to have a clear and obvious solution, and I do not intend to propose one. Instead, I should like to offer an attempt at analysing and conceptualizing them within a general framework.

The problems would seem to group themselves into three planes or levels, reflective of the three backgrounds against which the original poem, and any poem, manifests itself. First of all, as a message stated in words, a poem is set in a *linguistic context*: the poet, like any other formulator of a linguistic message, draws upon a part of the expressive means of the specific language he is using, in order to communicate something, and the words of the poem take on significance for the reader only when interpreted within that context. In the second place, a poem is written in interaction with a whole body of poetry existing within a given literary tradition, and the rhythm, metre, rhyme, and assonances of the poem, but also its imagery, themes, and *topoi*, are intimately linked with those in that whole array of other texts; in other words, the poem is set in what may be called a literary intertext. Finally, the poem exists within a socio-cultural situation, in which objects, symbols, and abstract concepts function in a way that is never exactly the same in any other society or culture. (It should be noted that this socio-cultural situation, though it finds expression in language, is something quite different from the linguistic context, and in fact the two frequently have different boundaries. It might be argued, for instance, that a country such as Belgium or Canada constitutes one socio-cultural situation but two linguistic contexts, while England and the United States form two socio-cultural situations but one linguistic context.)

The basic problem facing the translator of a poem, or at any rate the translator who takes it as his goal to create a text that is not only closely enough related to the original text to be called a translation but also meets the basic requirements for being called a poem in the new language he has taken as his "target", is that he must somehow "shift" the original poem not only to another linguistic context but almost without exception also to another literary intertext and socio-cultural situation. On each of these three planes, the choices confronting him range primarily on the axis "exoticizing" *versus* "naturalizing": should he retain a specific element of the original linguistic context (e.g. source-language syntax), the literary intertext (e.g. source-literature verse form), or the socio-cultural situation (e.g. source-culture symbols and images), knowing that in the new context, intertext, and situation that element will acquire an exotic aspect not attached to it in its native habitat? Or should he replace the element by one that he considers in some way matching or equivalent in the target context (e.g. target-language syntax), intertext (e.g. a target-literature verse form), or situation (e.g. a target-culture symbol or image)?

In the case of all but the most contemporary of poems, moreover, choices of this kind may be complicated by series of choices on another axis, that of "historicizing" *versus* "modernizing". Should the translator reflect the time of the original poem in his translation, selecting comparable historical solutions on the linguistic, literary, and socio-cultural planes, for instance resorting to equally archaic temporal dialect, poetic forms, and socio-cultural symbols? Or should he take advantage of the possibility offered by the fact of translation to "foreground" the relevancy which the original poem bore at the time it was written, before it was covered by the patina of history? Each translator of poetry, then, consciously or unconsciously works continually in various dimensions, making choices on each of three planes, the linguistic, the literary, and the socio-cultural, and on the x axis of exoticizing *versus* naturalizing and the y axis of historicizing versus modernizing.

What kinds of choices do translators actually make? Theorists have often argued that choices should be all of a piece: all exoticizing and historicizing, with an emphasis on *retention*, or all naturalizing and modernizing, with an emphasis on *re-creation*. In the eighteenth century, when the prevailing linguistic theory was that language was the garb of thought, and though languages differed, ideas were universal, Dr. Johnson could express the view that "[that translator] will deserve the highest praise, who ... can convey the same thoughts with the same graces, and who, when he translates, changes nothing but the language." At the other extreme are the followers of Ezra Pound, who in this century advocate "making it new" by means of "creative translation".

Both my own experience as a translator of poetry and the study and analysis of a large number of verse translations by others have convinced me that such "pure culture" translations are rarely if ever actually made. In practice, translators, Samuel Johnson and Ezra Pound among them, perform a series of pragmatic choices, here retentive, there re-creative, at this point historicizing or exoticizing, at that point modernizing or naturalizing, and emphasizing now this plane now that, at the cost of the other two. With the aid of a standard graph, the analyst can chart these choices in detail:

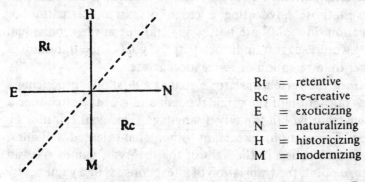

Rt = retentive
Rc = re-creative
E = exoticizing
N = naturalizing
H = historicizing
M = modernizing

for example, the graphs of the three versions "I went to Bommel for the bridge to see" (I), "I went to Bommel to see the bridge" (II), and "I went to Bommel to behold the bridge" (III) might be diagrammed as follows (C = linguistic context; I = literary intertext; S = socio-cultural situation):

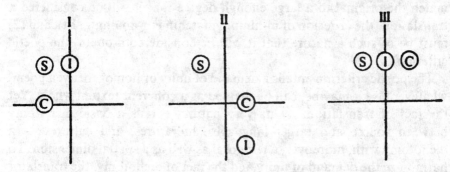

These graphs are fairly simple, since they have to do with only a single line. But with the same technique the entire series of solutions found in a specific translation of an entire poem can be diagrammed. In my experience, the graphs resulting from such experiments in analysis are always highly complex, reflecting as they do the complexity of the translator's choices.

There are a few generalizations that can be made on the basis of such analyses, and further research would probably lead to more. Among contemporary translators, for instance, there would seem to be a marked tendency towards modernization and naturalization of the linguistic context, paired with a similar but less clear tendency in the same direction in regard to the literary intertext, but an opposing tendency towards historicizing and exoticizing in the socio-cultural situation. The nineteenth century was much more inclined towards exoticizing and historicizing on all planes; the eighteenth, by and large, to modernizing and naturalizing even on the socio-cultural plane.

More important than such generalizations, though, is the fact that translators, even those advocating a credo of extreme retention or extreme re-creation, in reality are not at all clear-cut in their individual choices. This, I would suggest, indicates that the goal of the translator is something other than retention or re-creation as such.

Earlier I defined the verse translator's goal as a dual one: producing a text which is a translation of the original poem and is at the same time a poem in its own right within the target language. This goal can now be further defined. Translation, like many other goal-oriented activities, lends itself to consideration in the light of the theory of games. Viewed from this vantage point, the translation of a text consists of a game set by the translator: the game of producing an acceptable translation. It is a game with full rather than partial information, like chess as opposed to bridge, and a game against an imaginary opponent (or oneself, or nature), like patience as opposed to either chess or bridge. The two basic rules of the game of verse translation are that the final result (1) must match the original to a large enough degree that it will be considered a translation (the criterion of minimum matching or minimum fit), and (2) must be of such a nature that it will be considered a poem (the poetic criterion).

The poetic criterion entails a demand of unity or homogeneity: a poem, whatever else it may be, can be defined as a coherent textual whole. Yet the fact of translation, by its very nature, entails a basic dichotomy between source and target languages, literatures, and cultures — a dichotomy with, moreover, a temporal as well as a spatial dimension. To harmonize the demand of unity and the fact of dichotomy, the translator must resort to a game strategy of *illusionism*: accepting the dichotomy as inevitable, he must map out a general strategy of selecting from his retentive and re-creative possibilities those which will induce the illusion of unity. At the outset there are few further restrictions. But as the translator moves further into the game, each choice limits further choices: the choice of archaic idiom, for example, tends to prohibit later recourse to contemporary slang, and the choice of a strict rhyme scheme and/or metrical system serves to restrict subsequent lexical and syntactic choices quite severely.

Our problem, it would seem, has subtly shifted ground while we have been discussing it. Rather than coming to a definition of the limits of translatability such that we can say "all translation can attain this, and no more", we have arrived at a polyvalent situation: the verse translator, by virtue of the choices he is required to make in his pursuit of the illusion of unity, presents one possible interpretation (out of many) of the original poem, re-emphasizing certain aspects at the cost of others. It is for this reason that there will always be need of more than one translation of any poem of importance, since several translations present more facets of the original than any one can do.

Some poems and parts of poems, however, by the clusters of problems they present, seem to defy the translator in his attempts at achieving either an illusion or a minimum fit. In the case of Nijhoff's "De moeder de vrouw" I have never been able to win the translation game, time after time giving it up like a game of patience where neither kings nor aces turn up, because I could never find what seemed to me a satisfactory solution to the very first line. An English bridge at Bommel remains to be built.

A Note on Sources and Further Reading

Many of the terms used here are my own, at least as technical terms, but most of them have their histories. The categories linguistic context, literary intertext, and socio-cultural situation are closely akin to André Lefevere's textuality, intertextuality, and contextuality: see his "The Translation of Literature: An Approach", *Babel* (Avignon), 16 (1970), 75-79; his term intertextuality (and so, ultimately, my term intertext) derives from Julia Kristeva's concept of *intertextualité*. The notion of illusionism as a basic strategy of literary translation was introduced by the late Jiří Levý in his *Die literarische Übersetzung* (see below), pp. 31-32. Levý was also the first to recognize the relevance of the theory of games to the translatory act: see his "Translation as a Decision Process", in *To Honor Roman Jakobson* (3 vols.; The Hague: Mouton, 1967), 2, 1171-1182. The notion of matching as a concept describing more accurately than equivalence the relation between translation-linked text or parts of texts was suggested by Roy Harris in his "Translation Propositions", *Linguistica Antverpiensia*, 2 (1968), 217-227, see p. 221 n. 4. The related term fit, here first applied in the context of translation studies, is in wide use in a variety of other disciplines. The terminological pair *fable*/story and *sujet*/discourse constitute Tsvetan Todorov's French and Seymour Chatman's English equivalents of Boris Tomaševskij's original Russian terms; no doubt I have given them a broader use than Tomaševskij intended, since they were designed for narrative analysis only. The word foregrounding is the most common English translation of the Czech structuralist term *aktualisace*.

The line from Nijhoff's "De moeder de vrouw" is cited as first published, in the poet's *Nieuwe gedichten* (Amsterdam: Querido, 1934). The quotation from Samuel Johnson occurs in *The Idler*, No. 69 (11 August 1759); this number of *The Idler* and the preceding one form together a kind of encapsulated history of translation and translation theory from the ancients to Johnson's own day.

Of the many general studies on literary translation, the first that comes to mind, as the best brief survey of the subject, and the only one reflecting the present "state of the art" of translation studies, is unfortunately available solely in Slovak, so inaccessible to most readers. This is Anton Popovič's *Poetika umeleckého prekladu* (The Poetics of Literary Translation; [Bratislava]: Tatra, 1971). Jiří Levý's brilliant book *Die literarische Übersetzung: Theorie einer Kunstgattung* (Frankfurt am Main & Bonn: Athenäum, 1969; rev. tr. of *Umění překladu*, Prague: Československý spisovatel, 1963) is more comprehensive, but all in all it reflects an earlier stage of research.

Among other significant books in Western languages (I leave aside the many major studies in Russian), a great deal of valuable material is contained in three collections of conference papers, two of them American, one European: Reuben A. Brower (ed.), *On Translation* (Cambridge, Mass.: Harvard University Press, 1959; paperback repr. New York: Oxford University Press, 1966); William Arrowsmith and Roger Shattuck (eds.), *The Craft and Context of Translation: A Critical Symposium* (Austin: University of Texas Press, 1961; paperback repr. Garden City, N.Y.: Doubleday, 1964); and James S Holmes with Frans de Haan and Anton Popovič (eds.), *The Nature of Translation: Essays on the Theory and Practice of Literary Translation* (The Hague & Paris: Mouton and Bratislava: Publishing House of the Slovak Academy of Sciences, 1970).

"On Matching and Making Maps: From a Translator's Notebook" was published in the last issue of *Delta: A Review of Arts, Life, and Thought in the Netherlands* (Amsterdam), 16 (1973), No. 4, pp. 67-82. Reprinted in *Modern Poetry in Translation* (London), No. 26 (Autumn 1976), pp. 16-20.

On Matching and Making Maps: From a Translator's Notebook

The standard essay about the translation of poetry is a kind of under-baked cake whose batter was whipped together of half-truths and highly particular opinions. I hope that these notes do not conform to the recipe for the genre.

No translation of a poem is ever "the same as" the poem itself. It can't be, since everything about it is different: another language, another tradition, another author, another audience.

Nor is a translation of a poem really "equivalent" to its original, at least in any strict sense, however fashionable that term has become among the theorists of translation. Nowadays, after a generation of New Math in the schools, your average schoolchild needs only a drop of the figurative hat to list the qualities of an equivalence relationship. "Any relationship that is symmetrical, reflexive, and transitive", they will recite. And probably they can tell you just as easily why the translation relationship doesn't fill the bill.

Experiment. Put five pupils with a semester of algebra behind them onto the problem of multiplying $(x + y)$ and $(x - 2y)$. Then take twenty-five other pupils, and put five of them onto each of the five results, asking them to factor it out. The chances are pretty good that in the first round there will be five identical answers of $x^2 - xy - 2y^2$, and in the second twenty-five of $(x + y)(x - 2y)$ again. As it is only fair to expect in the case of a true equivalence relationship.

Now put five translators onto rendering even a syntactically straight-forward, metrically unbound, imagically simple poem like Carl Sandburg's "Fog" into, say, Dutch. The chances that any two of the five translations will be identical are very slight indeed. Then set twenty-five other translators into turning the five Dutch versions back into English, five translators to a version. Again, the result will almost certainly be as many renderings as there are translators. To call this equivalence is perverse.

"Equivalence", like "sameness", is asking too much. The languages and cultures to be bridged, however close they may sometimes seem, are too far apart and too disparately structured for true equivalence to be possible. What the translator strives for is, when you stop to think about it, not over-all sameness or equivalence, nor even local equivalence at the level of words or turns of phrase, rhythms or metres, images or musics. Rather it consists in finding what I should prefer to call "counterparts" or "matchings" — words, turns of phrase, and the rest, fulfilling functions in the language of the translation and the culture of its reader that in many and appropriate ways are closely akin (though never truly equivalent) to those of the words etc. in the language and culture of the original and its reader.

In seeking "counterparts" or "matchings", the translator is constantly faced by choices, choices he can make only on the basis of his individual grasp (knowledge, sensibility, experience...) of the two languages and cultures involved, and with the aid of his personal tastes and preferences.

It seems to me that there are two major levels or planes where choices are made. At the level of the poem as an entity, that of the "macrostructure", the translator finds that in selecting a specific counterpart for one aspect of the original poem, he may have made it impossible to find a satisfactory counterpart for another aspect. For instance, in choosing to use a metrical pattern and rhyme scheme matching that of the original more or less closely within the poetic conventions of the receptor culture, he may have worked himself into a position where he has to do considerable violence to the idiom of the poem, or even the over-all "content". If he is working from a more compact language to one that is less so, the result may be padding in the translation; if the other way round, he may have to omit what amounts to essential details. And even if the two languages are more or less of a length, the compulsions of the rhyme and metre will very likely lead him to introduce syntactic means and tonal qualities that have no counterpart in the original. If he tries to match the syntax and the tone, on the other hand, he may find himself faced with the necessity to abandon any attempt at finding an appropriate metrical or rhythmic counterpart.

A poem that leans very close to prose, with no strict metre, no complex development of imagery, no highly connotative use of language at various levels, may present few problems, and the translator will perhaps feel confident that he has succeeded in finding satisfactory matchings for every major aspect of the poem. But if the original is a highly complex structure exploiting a wide variety of possibilities in regard to metre, music, imagery, and idiom, together with a richness in ambiguities and tonalities, the translator can hardly avoid concluding that somewhere something has to yield.

Not much close attention has been paid, up to now, to the question of exactly how the translator makes these choices at the level of the macro-structure, selecting certain counterparts and rejecting others. More study has been made of his choices at the other major level, that of the individual word or group of words, the microstructural level: study, that is, of the translator's preference for one turn of phrase above another, his use of this image instead of that. But these lower-level choices are so largely circumscribed by the macrostructural that they are really second-ary. Faced with the choice between a word that appears to be an ideal match for the word in the original, but that has a syllable too many or an accent in the wrong place for the metre, and a word that is less appropriate in its meaning, overtones, or music, but that meets the metrical requirements, the translator who has decided to give priority to those requirements has to make do with the second word. (Translation is sometimes a more complex kind of scrabble. "Give me a common word of three syllables, with the accent on the first and the third, that begins with a *b* and means despair." Often, unfortunately, there just isn't a word to meet the requirements.) Of course the choice that forces itself upon a translator may fall so far short of the ideal that he decides to reshuffle his priorities completely and render the poem in quite a different way. Or for that matter give up entirely.

A case in point. For a while during the 1950s I was much intrigued as a translator by the challenge of Martinus Nijhoff's verse, which combines a strict form, usually that of the Italian sonnet, with an ease and naturalness of syntax and diction that border on the colloquial. The few translations of his poems into English that I had seen at that time had used a matching rhyme scheme and metre, but at the cost of introducing inversions and locutions that were quite out of keeping with Nijhoff's tone. Experi-menting, I discovered that by dropping the rhyme I could create enough verbal elbow-room within the sonnet metre and length for me to be able to produce versions of his poems that I felt adequately matched the meaning, the tone, and the subtle internal music of the originals. One of those sonnets is "Ad Infinitum," my translation of which seems to me to hearken closely to the Dutch poem in every way except that it does not rhyme. (Though there are a few individual words that I might try to find different solutions for if I were tackling the problem for the first time now.)

Some years later, in the mid-1960s, I wanted to include a version of Nijhoff's poem "De grot" in a number of *Delta* dealing with the Netherlands during the German occupation. This poem, though not quite a sonnet, presented much the same set of problems as other poems of

Nijhoff's I had translated earlier. More or less as a matter of course, I tried to apply the strategy I had evolved for the others. But after a great deal of trial-and-error I eventually had to conclude that in this case I couldn't make the strategy work. Some lines fitted quite naturally into the iambic-pentameter mould. But others were much too short (lines one and seven, for instance) or too long (line twelve); only dull circumlocutions or deliberate padding would solve the short lines, and only drastic excision the long. Still other lines (for example line three) were more or less the right length, but resisted my every effort to cage them in iambics.

Martinus Nijhoff, "Ad infinitum"   [1934]

De dienstmaagd giet van het geslachte lam
het bloed de schaal uit. Gij legt naast de haard
nieuw hout neer, vrouw, wier schoot mijn stem bewaart.
De spiegel blinkt. Het vlees hangt in de vlam.

Diep in het bos huilt een wolvin die baart,
en mijn stamvader die de deur inkwam
verheft wat hij als welp het nest uitnam
en nu een kind is, blank en onbehaard.

Wij staan één ogenblik, hij, ik, en 't wicht
dat aan zijn schouder leunt, naar dit vertrouwd
tafreel te zien: een wit vertrek, vol licht,

vol geur van vlees en pas getimmerd hout,
vol kort geluk, telkens opnieuw gesticht,
een hofstee op een open plek in 't woud.

Martinus Nijhoff, "De grot"   [1943]

Ik weet niet welke richting uit te gaan.
Het pad waarlangs wij kwamen stortte dicht,
en nergens voor ons zien wij eenig licht
wijzend een weg uit deze grot vandaan.

Elkaars naam roepend, houden wij verband.
Water, dat neerdruipt van boven ons hoofd,
heeft onze laatste toortsen uitgedoofd.
De hand tast voorwaarts langs de klamme wand.

Het eene uur na 't andere gaat om.
En menig onzer denkt aan blauwe lucht,
doortinteld van blij vogelengerucht
en 't nooit genoeg aanschouwde licht der zon.

Till suddenly I realized that by dropping my attempt at metrical matching and concentrating on other aspects, I could produce a poem that might be effective in a quite different manner. The result is, in one way, not Nijhoff — he would have been taken aback by it, as I'm confident he would not have been by the experiment of the rhymeless sonnets. But in another, very real way it is him: a kind of younger, latter-generation Nijhoff liberated from the shackles of received forms, paradoxically applying the free-verse techniques of the post-war Dutch poets to give expression to the dark predicament of caged and fettered man in the midst of the war.

Martinus Nijhoff, "Ad Infinitum"   [1961]

The servant girl throws out the slaughtered lamb's
blood from the bowl. You lay new wood beside
the hearth, woman whose womb my voice preserves.
The mirror gleams. The meat hangs in the flame.

Deep in the woods a bearing she-wolf cries,
and my forefather who came in the door
lifts up what he took from the lair as whelp
and now's become a child, pale, without hair.

We stand one moment, he, I, and the tot
leaning on his shoulder, and gaze at this
familiar scene: a white room, filled with light,

filled with the smell of meat and new-sawn wood,
filled with brief joy constantly formed anew,
a homestead on a clearing in the woods.

Martinus Nijhoff, "The Cave"   [1965]

I don't know which way to turn.
The path we came by has filled in,
and nowhere ahead of us is there any light
pointing a way out of this cave.

We keep in touch by calling each other's names.
Water dripping from above our heads
has put out our last torches.
Hands feel forwards along the damp wall.

The hours pass one by one.
And our thoughts are full of blue sky
a-twinkle with glad birdsong
and the never-sufficiently-looked-at light of the sun.

Some day another translator (or even I) may work out another version of "De grot" in English that does justice to its formal structure. If he succeeds in this without inflicting greater damage upon the other aspects of the poem than I have done, his translation will deserve to supplant mine. More probably, the two will continue to exist side by side, each supplementing the other as a somewhat differently faceted commentary on the many-faceted original.

That is the usual situation, for there are no "perfect" translations, few that even approach "perfection." (It's the same old "equivalence" problem.) Some are better, some worse, but almost all succeed in matching certain aspects of the original quite closely, and others only more remotely if at all. To borrow an image from general semantics, all translations are maps, the territories are the originals. And just as no single map of a territory is suitable for every purpose, so is there no "definitive" translation of a poem. What we need is a variety of inevitably less-than-definitive versions for a variety of purposes: strictly metrical translations, perhaps, but also free-verse renderings, prose ponies, even glosses *cum* commentaries, each of them a map which in its own way can help us to reconnoitre the territory better. The explicatory method developed by Stanley Burnshaw in his anthology *The Poem Itself* can be very useful; so too can the technique of juxtaposing a series of verse translations of the same poem, as was done in the Summer 1971 issue of *Delta* for M. Vasalis' "De weg terug."

Lucebert, "School der poëzie"　　[1952]

Ik ben geen lieflijke dichter
Ik ben de schielijke oplichter
Der liefde, zie onder haar de haat
En daarop een kaaklende daad.

Lyriek is de moeder der politiek,
Ik ben niets dan omroeper van oproer
En mijn mystiek is het bedorven voer
Van leugen waarmee de deugd zich uitziekt.

Ik bericht, dat de dichters van fluweel
Schuw en humanisties dood gaan.
Voortaan zal de hete ijzeren keel
Der ontroerde beulen muzikaal opengaan.

Nog ik, die in deze bundel woon
Als een rat in de val, snak naar het riool
Van revolutie en roep: rijmratten, hoon,
Hoon nog deze veel te schone poëzieschool.

However poor or rich the translation, the poem itself remains, a territory to be mapped by another translator (or the same translator, discontent) another day.

Occasionally things work out differently. Two languages can chance to "interlock" at specific points, quite accidentally, in such a fashion that the translation appears to come through more or less all of a piece. This happens all too rarely, but when it does, the translation seems almost to write itself. One case in my experience was Lucebert's "School der poëzie," where English presented matching rhymes almost for the taking, and rhymes with (it seemed to me) a kind of unexpected inevitability very similar to that of the rhymes in the Dutch. Even much of the alliteration and assonance was ready to hand in English, almost impossible to miss. This, of course, is a fluke of fate; a translator trying to render the same poem into, say, French might throw up his hands in despair.

Another poem in which this kind of linguistic "interlocking" seemed to be working to my advantage as a translator was Gerrit Achterberg's "Glazenwasser." True, this is not such a clear-cut case as Lucebert's poem: the ascension/aspiration rhyme is not entirely satisfactory, nor is the combination "supramundance aspiration" as a rendering of *hemel-zucht*. And "universe and all" is none too felicitous as a double translation of the Dutch *heelal*. But for large parts of the poem the pieces

Lucebert, "School of Poetry"   [1963]

I'm not some lovable rime-spook
I am the expeditious crook
Of love, see the hate beneath
And upon it a cackling deed.

Lyrics are the parents of politics,
I am merely the reporter of revolt
And my mysticism is the spoilt
Lie-fodder virtue swallows when it's sick.

I announce that the velvet poets
Are shyly and humanistically dying.
Henceforth the impassioned torturers, vying
Musically, shall swell their hot iron throats.

And I, who live in this book of verse
Like a rat in a trap, long for the sewer
Of revolution and roar: rime-rats, jeer,
Jeer at this much too lovely school of verse.

seemed to fit together almost effortlessly to form a translation that matched the taut, compact original in a surprising number of ways.

That is, until I discovered some time later (I had worked on the translation from a typed-over text of the original) that the fifth line in the Dutch does not read "Handen- en voeten*val*" (as my typescript had had it) but "Handen- en voeten*tal*." I still see no way of fitting that -*tal* (number) into a formally counterparted translation. But I like the translation as it is, a rendering with a flaw, like the grain of sand in a cultured pearl, but for all that not a bad English poem (to my taste, at any rate).

Mistakes of this kind are not really as important as they are often made out to be. At least as long as they are incidental, and do not make logical or poetic nonsense out of the poem as a whole. For that matter, translation "errors" on even a more than incidental scale have been a not unimportant factor in the enrichment of literatures and cultures, over the centuries. Not that translators should take encouragement from that to go forth and err once more. But it's something of a solace.

That translating poetry is largely a matter of making choices between less-than-perfect possibilities is illustrated in another way by my rendering of Paul Snoek's "Rustiek landschapje." Several years ago, in an essay titled "Poem and Metapoem," I tried to describe what I felt was the major problem involved in translating this poem, and to outline how I had attempted to solve it. The passage seems relevant enough to cite.

A fundamental theme of the Dutch poem is the juxtaposition of ganzen *(geese) and* onze tantes *(our aunts), with such descriptive terms as* waggelen, wandelen, worden... oud, *and* kwakende *applying to both.*

Gerrit Achterberg, "Glazenwasser"   [1949]

Hij laat zichzelve leunen in het licht.
Zijn lichaam houdt heelal.
Om hem is elke val
met hemelvaart in evenwicht.

Handen- en voetental
verrichten in de lucht
een klein gebarenspel, een klucht
die hij alleen begrijpen zal;
het mene tekel en getal
van roekeloze hemelzucht.

These juxtaposed and coalescing images (suddenly separated again in the two "clues" which close the poem, turning it into a picture puzzle) are reinforced acoustically by a complex system of alliteration and internal rhyme.

A low-rank translation of the opening line would yield "The geese are like our aunts" or a similar rendering. But that lacks the acoustic complexity of the Dutch. Moreover it leads the translator to the further problem that in English geese do not quack (see line fourteen) but honk or possibly hiss. Retention of the geese leads to honking relatives, and that to a suggestion, disturbingly inappropriate in this context, of honking car-horns. Retention of the quacking, on the other hand, leads from geese to ducks. A choice for ducks and quacking instead of honking and geese opens up the possibility of turning the aunts into cousins and so to beginning the [translation] with the initial elements for an acoustic system parallel to that of the Dutch ("De ganzen zijn net onze tantes..."; "The ducks are like our cousins..."). This choice, however, leaves the human image less concrete at the end of the first line than in the Dutch, since cousins, unlike aunts, are of unspecified sex and relative age; the translator who has given preference to this series of choices must rely on the rest of the first stanza, reinforced by the last, to make it clear that the cousins, too, are female and growing old. In other words the major cluster of choices facing the translator of this poem is that of either reconstructing the acoustic qualities of the Dutch at the cost of shifting the nature of two of the poem's major images (though preserving the nature of their juxtaposition) or retaining the images at the cost of introducing alien implications with the "honking" and failing to parallel the acoustic qualities of the poem.

These notes are among the last bits of copy to be turned in before the

Gerrit Achterberg, "Window Washer"   [1958]

He lets himself lean in the light.
His body holds the universe and all.
Around him every fall
is balanced by ascension.

Footfall and hand-
fall act a sparse
pantomime in the air, a farce
that he alone can understand;
the mene tekel and the numeral
of reckless supramundane aspiration.

final issue of *Delta* goes to press. Seventeen years ago, when Ed. Hoornik, Hans van Marle, and I first sat together in an attic room in Amsterdam South, making plans for an English-language review of Dutch "arts, life, and thought," there was very little contemporary Dutch poetry available in English. An older generation of translators from the Dutch — people such as Sir Herbert Grierson, A.J. Barnouw, and Pieter Geyl — had largely turned to other, more "serious" pursuits, and even in their days of major activity in translating their chief concern had been with older poets. James Brockway and I were, I think, the only ones who were more than incidentally interested in translating contemporary Dutch poetry.

In the years since then, it is safe to say that more Dutch verse, or at least "lyric" verse, has been rendered into English than ever before. Some of it is to be found in anthologies or special numbers of literary magazines devoted specifically to writing from the Low Countries, some scattered through the pages of dozens of reviews, "little" or not so little, some in even more fugitive publications, from program notes to posters. But a sizable amount of it has been published within the pages of *Delta*. Largely by default, much of this was in my English. But quite a range of other translators also were presented, from Jack Hirschman and Christopher Levenson to Koos Schuur and Marjolijn de Jager.

Paul Snoek, "Rustiek landschapje"   [1959]

De ganzen zijn net onze tantes:
zij waggelen en wandelen
en worden watertandend
in de modder oud.

Maar plots doet een geweldig
knalletje hun landelijke,
liefelijke vliezen bijna scheuren.

Dat was een hereboer natuurlijk:
hij schiet met loden spek,
de gek. Hij sneed een appel
in de bek en riep spierrood
van ontspanning: "Ik mest,
jawel, ik mest een gulden peer".

Of die kwakende tantes moesten lachen.
1. Zij snoeien hun rozen
met een kromgekweekt mes;
2. Hoe oud zijn de ganzen?

Today, as *Delta* leaves the scene, a younger generation of translators is seeking and finding attention for Dutch poetry in the English-speaking (or, better, English-reading) countries. Peter Nijmeijer in England and Larry Ten Harmsel in America come first to mind, but there are a number of others. They form a warranty that there is a future for Dutch poetry in English, even if *Delta* will no longer be there to provide its offices as intermediary.

Meanwhile, there is still no full-scale, book-size anthology of modern or contemporary Dutch poetry (though one is rumoured to be in the making). As for earlier verse, Barnouw's historical anthology is a quarter of a century old, and was in fact outdated even when it appeared. The "classic" Dutch poets of the seventeenth century and those of the reawakening in the late nineteenth are represented by a mere handful of widely scattered and largely forgotten renderings. (The only exception is, surprisingly enough, the metaphysical Revius — thanks to the energies of Henrietta Ten Harmsel.) And no one has done justice to more than a very few of the tenderly beautiful lyrics and ballads of the Dutch Middle Ages. There is, then, more than enough yet to be done. And more than enough that is rewarding for the translator to do, despite his ever present awareness that

Paul Snoek, "Rustic Landscape"   [1965]

The ducks are like our cousins:
they waggle and walk
and slavering at the mouth
in the mud grow old.

But all at once a terrific
bang almost breaks
their pleasant peasant membranes.

That was the farmer himself of course:
he's trying the shotgun out,
the lout. He cut an apple
in the snout and cried, stark red
with relief: "I'm dressing,
yes, a golden pear."

And did those quacking cousins have a laugh.
(1) They prune their roses
with a crooked knife;
(2) How old are the ducks?

no matter how hard he may try, not even the optimum translation can ever fully and entirely match its original, ever be more than a map of it. The territory remains, though it must not remain *terra incognita*.

Part Two:
Studying Translation
and Translation Studies

"The Name and Nature of Translation Studies" is an expanded version of a paper presented in the Translation Section of the Third International Congress of Applied Linguistics, held in Copenhagen, 21-26 August 1972. First issued in the APPTS series of the Translation Studies Section, Department of General Literary Studies, University of Amsterdam, 1972, presented here in its second pre-publication form (1975). A slightly different version appeared in *Indian Journal of Applied Linguistics*, 13 (1987), pp. 9-24. A Dutch translation was published under the title "Wat is vertaalwetenschap?" in Bernard T. Tervoort (ed.), *Wetenschap & Taal: Het verschijnsel taal van verschillende zijden benaderd* (Muiderberg: Coutinho, 1977), pp. 148-165.

The Name and Nature of Translation Studies[1]

1.1

"Science", Michael Mulkay points out, "tends to proceed by means of discovery of new areas of ignorance."[2] The process by which this takes place has been fairly well defined by the sociologists of science and research.[3] As a new problem or set of problems comes into view in the world of learning, there is an influx of researchers from adjacent areas, bringing with them the paradigms and models that have proved fruitful in their own fields. These paradigms and models are then brought to bear on the new problem, with one of two results. In some situations the problem proves amenable to explicitation, analysis, explication, and at least partial solution within the bounds of one of the paradigms or models, and in that case it is annexed as a legitimate branch of an established field of study. In other situations the paradigms or models fail to produce sufficient results, and researchers become aware that new methods are needed to approach the problem.

In this second type of situation, the result is a tension between researchers investigating the new problem and colleagues in their former fields, and this tension can gradually lead to the establishment of new channels of communication and the development of what has been called a new disciplinary utopia, that is, a new sense of a shared interest in a common set of problems, approaches, and objectives on the part of a new grouping of researchers. As W.O. Hagstrom has indicated, these two steps, the establishment of communication channels and the development of a disciplinary utopia, "make it possible for scientists to identify with the emerging discipline and to claim legitimacy for their point of view when appealing to university bodies or groups in the larger society."[4]

1.2

Though there are no doubt a few scholars who would object, particularly among the linguists, it would seem to me clear that in regard to the complex of problems clustered round the phenomenon of translating and translations,[5] the second situation now applies. After centuries of incidental and desultory attention from a scattering of authors, philologians, and literary scholars, plus here and there a theologian or an idiosyncratic linguist, the subject of translation has enjoyed a marked and constant increase in interest on the part of scholars in recent years, with the Second World War as a kind of turning point. As this interest has solidified and expanded, more and more scholars have moved into the field, particularly from the adjacent fields of linguistics, linguistic philosophy, and literary studies, but also from such seemingly more remote disciplines as information theory, logic, and mathematics, each of them carrying with him paradigms, quasi-paradigms, models, and methodologies that he felt could be brought to bear on this new problem.

At first glance, the resulting situation today would appear to be one of great confusion, with no consensus regarding the types of models to be tested, the kinds of methods to be applied, the varieties of terminology to be used. More than that, there is not even likemindedness about the contours of the field, the problem set, the discipline as such. Indeed, scholars are not so much as agreed on the very name for the new field.

Nevertheless, beneath the superficial level, there are a number of indications that for the field of research focusing on the problems of translating and translations Hagstrom's disciplinary utopia is taking shape. If this is a salutary development (and I believe that it is), it follows that it is worth our while to further the development by consciously turning our attention to matters that are serving to impede it.

1.3

One of these impediments is the lack of appropriate channels of communication. For scholars and researchers in the field, the channels that do exist still tend to run via the older disciplines (with their attendant norms in regard to models, methods, and terminology), so that papers on the subject of translation are dispersed over periodicals in a wide variety of scholarly fields and journals for practising translators. It is clear that there is a need for other communication channels, cutting across the traditional disciplines to reach all scholars working in the field, from whatever background.

2.1

But I should like to focus our attention on two other impediments to the development of a disciplinary utopia. The first of these, the lesser of the two in importance, is the seemingly trivial matter of the name for this field of research. It would not be wise to continue referring to the discipline by its subject matter as has been done at this conference, for the map, as the General Semanticists constantly remind us, is not the territory, and failure to distinguish the two can only further confusion.

Through the years, diverse terms have been used in writings dealing with translating and translations, and one can find references in English to "the art" or "the craft" of translation, but also to the "principles" of translation, the "fundamentals" or the "philosophy". Similar terms recur in French and German. In some cases the choice of term reflects the attitude, point of approach, or background of the writer; in others it has been determined by the fashion of the moment in scholarly terminology.

There have been a few attempts to create more "learned" terms, most of them with the highly active disciplinary suffix -ology. Roger Goffin, for instance, has suggested the designation "translatology" in English, and either its cognate or *traductologie* in French.[6] But since the -ology suffix derives from Greek, purists reject a contamination of this kind, all the more so when the other element is not even from Classical Latin, but from Late Latin in the case of *translatio* or Renaissance French in that of *traduction*. Yet Greek alone offers no way out, for "metaphorology", "metaphraseology", or "metaphrastics" would hardly be of aid to us in making our subject clear even to university bodies, let alone to other "groups in the larger society."[7] Such other terms as "translatistics" or "translistics", both of which have been suggested, would be more readily understood, but hardly more acceptable.

2.21

Two further, less classically constructed terms have come to the fore in recent years. One of these began its life in a longer form, "the theory of translating" or "the theory of translation" (and its corresponding forms: "Theorie des Übersetzens", "théorie de la traduction"). In English (and in German) it has since gone the way of many such terms, and is now usually compressed into "translation theory" (*Übersetzungstheorie*). It has been a productive designation, and can be even more so in future, but only if it is restricted to its proper meaning. For, as I hope to make clear in the course of this paper, there is much valuable study and research being done in the discipline, and a need for much more to be done, that does not, strictly speaking, fall within the scope of theory formation.

2.22

The second term is one that has, to all intents and purposes, won the field in German as a designation for the entire discipline.[8] This is the term *Übersetzungswissenschaft*, constructed to form a parallel to *Sprach-wissenschaft*, *Literaturwissenschaft*, and many other *Wissenschaften*. In French, the comparable designation, "science de la traduction", has also gained ground, as have parallel terms in various other languages.

One of the first to use a parallel-sounding term in English was Eugene Nida, who in 1964 chose to entitle his theoretical handbook *Towards a Science of Translating*.[9] It should be noted, though, that Nida did not intend the phrase as a name for the entire field of study, but only for one aspect of the *process* of translating as such.[10] Others, most of them not native speakers of English, have been more bold, advocating the term "science of translation" (or "translation science") as the appropriate designation for this emerging discipline as a whole. Two years ago this recurrent suggestion was followed by something like canonization of the term when Bausch, Klegraf, and Wilss took the decision to make it the main title to their analytical bibliography of the entire field.[11]

It was a decision that I, for one, regret. It is not that I object to the term *Übersetzungswissenschaft*, for there are few if any valid arguments against that designation for the subject in German. The problem is not that the discipline is not a *Wissenschaft*, but that not all *Wissenschaften* can properly be called sciences. Just as no one today would take issue with the terms *Sprachwissenschaft* and *Literaturwissenschaft*, while more than a few would question whether linguistics has yet reached a stage of precision, formalization, and paradigm formation such that it can properly be described as a science, and while practically everyone would agree that literary studies are not, and in the foreseeable future will not be, a science in any true sense of the English word, in the same way I question whether we can with any justification use a designation for the study of translating and translations that places it in the company of mathematics, physics, and chemistry, or even biology, rather than that of sociology, history, and philosophy — or for that matter of literary studies.

2.3

There is, however, another term that is active in English in the naming of new disciplines. This is the word "studies". Indeed, for disciplines that within the old distinction of the universities tend to fall under the humanities or arts rather than the sciences as fields of learning, the word would seem to be almost as active in English as the word *Wissenschaft* in German. One need only think of Russian studies, American studies, Commonwealth studies, population studies, communication studies. True, the word raises a few new complications, among them the fact that it is difficult to derive an adjectival form. Nevertheless, the designation "translation studies" would seem to be the most appropriate of all those available in English, and its adoption as the standard term for the discipline as a whole would remove a fair amount of confusion and misunderstanding. I shall set the example by making use of it in the rest of this paper.

3

A greater impediment than the lack of a generally accepted name in the way of the development of translation studies is the lack of any general consensus as to the scope and structure of the discipline. What constitutes the field of translation studies? A few would say it coincides with comparative (or contrastive) terminological and lexicographical studies; several look upon it as practically identical with comparative or contrastive linguistics; many would consider it largely synonymous with translation theory. But surely it is different, if not always distinct, from the first two of these, and more than the third. As is usually to be found in the case of emerging disciplines, there has as yet been little meta-reflection on the nature of translation studies as such — at least that has made its way into print and to my attention. One of the few cases that I have found is that of Werner Koller, who has given the following delineation of the subject: "Übersetzungswissenschaft ist zu verstehen als Zusammenfassung und Überbegriff für alle Forschungsbemühungen, die von den Phänomenen 'Übersetzen' und 'Übersetzung' ausgehen oder auf diese Phänomene zielen." (Translation studies is to be understood as a collective and inclusive designation for all research activities taking the phenomena of translating and translation as their basis or focus.[12])

3.1

From this delineation it follows that translation studies is, as no one I suppose would deny, an empirical discipline. Such disciplines, it has often been pointed out, have two major objectives, which Carl G. Hempel has phrased as "to describe particular phenomena in the world of our experience and to establish general principles by means of which they can be explained and predicted."[13] As a field of pure research — that is to say, research pursued for its own sake, quite apart from any direct practical application outside its own terrain — translation studies thus has two main objectives: (1) to describe the phenomena of translating and translation(s) as they manifest themselves in the world of our experience, and (2) to establish general principles by means of which these phenomena can be explained and predicted. The two branches of pure translation studies concerning themselves with these objectives can be designated *descriptive translation studies* (DTS) or *translation description* (TD) and *theoretical translation studies* (ThTS) or *translation theory* (TTh).

3.11

Of these two, it is perhaps appropriate to give first consideration to *descriptive translation studies*, as the branch of the discipline which constantly maintains the closest contact with the empirical phenomena under study. There would seem to be three major kinds of research in DTS, which may be distinguished by their focus as product-oriented, function-oriented, and process-oriented.

3.111

Product-oriented DTS, that area of research which describes existing translations, has traditionally been an important area of academic research in translation studies. The starting point for this type of study is the description of individual translations, or text-focused translation description. A second phase is that of comparative translation description, in which comparative analyses are made of various translations of the same text, either in a single language or in various languages. Such individual and comparative descriptions provide the materials for surveys of larger corpuses of translations, for instance those made within a specific period, language, and/or text or discourse type. In practice the corpus has usually been restricted in all three ways: seventeenth-century literary translations into French, or medieval English Bible translations. But such descriptive surveys can also be larger in scope, diachronic as well as (approximately) synchronic, and one of the eventual goals of product-oriented DTS might possibly be a general history of translations — however ambitious such a goal may sound at this time.

3.112

Function-oriented DTS is not interested in the description of translations in themselves, but in the description of their function in the recipient socio-cultural situation: it is a study of contexts rather than texts. Pursuing such questions as which texts were (and, often as important, were not) translated at a certain time in a certain place, and what influences were exerted in consequence, this area of research is one that has attracted less concentrated attention than the area just mentioned, though it is often introduced as a kind of sub-theme or counter-theme in histories of translations and in literary histories. Greater emphasis on it could lead to the development of a field of translation sociology (or — less felicitous but more accurate, since it is a legitimate area of translation studies as well as of sociology — socio-translation studies).

3.113

Process-oriented DTS concerns itself with the process or act of translation itself. The problem of what exactly takes place in the "little black box" of the translator's "mind" as he creates a new, more or less matching text in another language has been the subject of much speculation on the part of translation's theorists, but there has been very little attempt at systematic investigation of this process under laboratory conditions. Admittedly, the process is an unusually complex one, one which, if I.A. Richards is correct, "may very probably be the most complex type of event yet produced in the evolution of the cosmos."[14] But psychologists have developed and are developing highly sophisticated methods for analysing and describing other complex mental processes, and it is to be hoped that in future this problem, too, will be given closer attention, leading to an area of study that might be called translation psychology or psycho-translation studies.

3.12

The other main branch of pure translation studies, *theoretical translation studies* or *translation theory*, is, as its name implies, not interested in describing existing translations, observed translation functions, or experimentally determined translating processes, but in using the results of descriptive translation studies, in combination with the information available from related fields and disciplines, to evolve principles, theories, and models which will serve to explain and predict what translating and translations are and will be.

3.121

The ultimate goal of the translation theorist in the broad sense must undoubtedly be to develop a full, inclusive theory accommodating so many elements that it can serve to explain and predict all phenomena falling within the terrain of translating and translation, to the exclusion of all phenomena falling outside it. It hardly needs to be pointed out that a *general translation theory* in such a true sense of the term, if indeed it is achievable, will necessarily be highly formalized and, however the scholar may strive after economy, also highly complex.

Most of the theories that have been produced to date are in reality little more than prolegomena to such a general translation theory. A good share of them, in fact, are not actually theories at all, in any scholarly sense of the term, but an array of axioms, postulates, and hypotheses that are so formulated as to be both too inclusive (covering also non-translatory acts and non-translations) and too exclusive (shutting out some translatory acts and some works generally recognized as translations).

3.122

Others, though they too may bear the designation of "general" translation theories (frequently preceded by the scholar's protectively cautious "towards") are in fact not general theories, but partial or specific in their scope, dealing with only one or a few of the various aspects of translation theory as a whole. It is in this area of partial theories that the most significant advances have been made in recent years, and in fact it will probably be necessary for a great deal of further research to be conducted in them before we can even begin to think about arriving at a true general theory in the sense I have just outlined. *Partial translation theories* are specified in a number of ways. I would suggest, though, that they can be grouped together into six main kinds.

3.1221

First of all, there are translation theories that I have called, with a somewhat unorthodox extension of the term, *medium-restricted translation theories*, according to the medium that is used. Medium-restricted theories can be further subdivided into theories of translation as performed by humans (human translation), as performed by computers (machine translation), and as performed by the two in conjunction (mixed or machine-aided translation). Human translation breaks down into (and restricted theories or "theories" have been developed for) oral translation or interpreting (with the further distinction between consecutive and simultaneous) and written translation. Numerous examples of valuable research into machine and machine-aided translation are no doubt familiar to us all, and perhaps also several into oral human translation. That examples of medium-restricted theories of written translation do not come to mind so easily is largely owing to the fact that their authors have the tendency to present them in the guise of unmarked or general theories.

3.1222

Second, there are theories that are area-restricted. *Area-restricted theories* can be of two closely related kinds; restricted as to the languages involved or, which is usually not quite the same, and occasionally hardly at all, as to the cultures involved. In both cases, language restriction and culture restriction, the degree of actual limitation can vary. Theories are feasible for translation between, say, French and German (language-pair restricted theories) as opposed to translation within Slavic languages (language-group restricted theories) or from Romance languages to Germanic languages (language-group pair restricted theories). Similarly, theories might at least hypothetically be developed for translation within Swiss culture (one-culture restricted), or for translation between Swiss and Belgian cultures (cultural-pair restricted), as opposed to translation within western Europe (cultural-group restricted) or between languages reflecting a pre-technological culture and the languages of contemporary Western culture (cultural-group pair restricted). Language-restricted theories have close affinities with the work being done in comparative linguistics and stylistics (though it must always be remembered that a language-pair translation grammar must be a different thing from a contrastive grammar developed for the purpose of language acquisition). In the field of culture-restricted theories there has been little detailed research, though culture restrictions, by being confused with language restrictions, sometimes get introduced into language-restricted theories, where they are out of place in all but those rare cases where culture and language boundaries coincide in both the source and target situations. It is moreover no doubt true that some aspects of theories that are presented as general in reality pertain only to the Western cultural area.

3.1223

Third, there are *rank-restricted theories*, that is to say, theories that deal with discourses or texts as wholes, but concern themselves with lower linguistic ranks or levels. Traditionally, a great deal of writing on translation was concerned almost entirely with the rank of the word, and the word and the word group are still the ranks at which much terminologically-oriented thinking about scientific and technological translation takes place. Most linguistically-oriented research, on the other hand, has until very recently taken the sentence as its upper rank limit, largely ignoring the macro-structural aspects of entire texts as translation problems. The clearly discernible trend away from sentential linguistics in the direction of textual linguistics will, it is to be hoped, encourage linguistically-oriented theorists to move beyond sentence-restricted translation theories to the more complex task of developing text-rank (or "rank-free") theories.

3.1224

Fourth, there are *text-type* (or discourse-type) *restricted theories*, dealing with the problem of translating specific types or genres of lingual messages. Authors and literary scholars have long concerned themselves with the problems intrinsic to translating literary texts or specific genres of literary texts; theologians, similarly, have devoted much attention to questions of how to translate the Bible and other sacred works. In recent years some effort has been made to develop a specific theory for the translation of scientific texts. All these studies break down, however, because we still lack anything like a formal theory of message, text, or discourse types. Both Bühler's theory of types of communication, as further developed by the Prague structuralists, and the definitions of language varieties arrived at by linguists particularly of the British school provide material for criteria in defining text types that would lend themselves to operationalization more aptly than the inconsistent and mutually contradictory definitions or traditional genre theories. On the other hand, the traditional theories cannot be ignored, for they continue to play a large part in creating the expectation criteria of translation readers. Also requiring study is the important question of text-type skewing or shifting in translation.

3.1225

Fifth, there are *time-restricted theories*, which fall into two types: theories regarding the translation of contemporary texts, and theories having to do with the translation of texts from an older period. Again there would seem to be a tendency to present one of the theories, that having to do with contemporary texts, in the guise of a general theory; the other, the theory of what can perhaps best be called cross-temporal translation, is a matter that has led to much disagreement, particularly among literarily oriented theorists, but to few generally valid conclusions.

3.1226

Finally, there are *problem-restricted theories*, theories which confine themselves to one or more specific problems within the entire area of general translation theory, problems that can range from such broad and basic questions as the limits of variance and invariance in translation or the nature of translation equivalence (or, as I should prefer to call it, translation matching) to such more specific matters as the translation of metaphors or of proper names.

3.123

It should be noted that theories can frequently be restricted in more than one way. Contrastive linguists interested in translation, for instance, will probably produce theories that are not only language-restricted but rank- and time-restricted, having to do with translations between specific pairs of contemporary temporal dialects at sentence rank. The theories of literary scholars, similarly, usually are restricted as to medium and text type, and generally also as to culture group; they normally have to do with written texts within the (extended) Western literary tradition. This does not necessarily reduce the worth of such partial theories, for even a theoretical study restricted in every way — say a theory of the manner in which subordinate clauses in contemporary German novels should be translated into written English — can have implications for the more general theory towards which scholars must surely work. It would be wise, though, not to lose sight of such a truly general theory, and wiser still not to succumb to the delusion that a body of restricted theories — for instance, a complex of language-restricted theories of how to translate sentences — can be an adequate substitute for it.

3.2

After this rapid overview of the two main branches of pure research in translation studies, I should like to turn to that branch of the discipline which is, in Bacon's words, "of use" rather than "of light": applied translation studies.[15]

3.21

In this discipline, as in so many others, the first thing that comes to mind when one considers the applications that extend beyond the limits of the discipline itself is that of teaching. Actually, the teaching of translating is of two types which need to be carefully distinguished. In the one case, translating has been used for centuries as a technique in foreign-language teaching and a test of foreign-language acquisition. I shall return to this type in a moment. In the second case, a more recent phenomenon, translating is taught in schools and courses to train professional translators. This second situation, that of *translator training*, has raised a number of questions that fairly cry for answers: questions that have to do primarily with teaching methods, testing techniques, and curriculum planning. It is obvious that the search for well-founded, reliable answers to these questions constitutes a major area (and for the time being, at least, *the* major area) of research in applied translation studies.

3.22

A second, closely related area has to do with the needs for translation aids, both for use in translator training and to meet the requirements of the practising translator. The needs are many and various, but fall largely into two classes: (1) lexicographical and terminological aids and (2) grammars. Both these classes of aids have traditionally been provided by scholars in other, related disciplines, and it could hardly be argued that work on them should be taken over *in toto* as areas of applied translation studies. But lexicographical aids often fall far short of translation needs, and contrastive grammars developed for language-acquisition purposes are not really an adequate subsitute for variety-marked translation-matching grammars. There would seem to be a need for scholars in applied translation studies to clarify and define the specific requirements that aids of these kinds should fulfil if they are to meet the needs of practising and prospective translators, and to work together with lexicologists and contrastive linguists in developing them.

3.23

A third area of applied translation studies is that of *translation policy*. The task of the translation scholar in this area is to render informed advice to others in defining the place and role of translators, translating, and translations in society at large: such questions, for instance, as determining what works need to be translated in a given socio-cultural situation, what the social and economic position of the translator is and should be, or (and here I return to the point raised above) what part translating should play in the teaching and learning of foreign languages. In regard to that last policy question, since it should hardly be the task of translation studies to abet the use of translating in places where it is dysfunctional, it would seem to me that priority should be given to extensive and rigorous research to assess the efficacy of translating as a technique and testing method in language learning. The chance that it is not efficacious would appear to be so great that in this case it would seem imperative for program research to be preceded by policy research.

3.24

A fourth, quite different area of applied translation studies is that of *translation criticism*. The level of such criticism is today still frequently very low, and in many countries still quite uninfluenced by developments within the field of translation studies. Doubtless the activities of translation interpretation and evaluation will always elude the grasp of objective analysis to some extent, and so continue to reflect the intuitive, impressionist attitudes and stances of the critic. But closer contact between translation scholars and translation critics could do a great deal to reduce the intuitive element to a more acceptable level.

3.31

After this brief survey of the main branches of translation studies, there are two further points that I should like to make. The first is this: in what has preceded, descriptive, theoretical, and applied translation studies have been presented as three fairly distinct branches of the entire discipline, and the order of presentation might be taken to suggest that their import for one another is unidirectional, translation description supplying the basic data upon which translation theory is to be built, and the two of them providing the scholarly findings which are to be put to use in applied translation studies. In reality, of course, the relation is a dialectical one, with each of the three branches supplying materials for the other two, and making use of the findings which they in turn provide it. Translation theory, for instance, cannot do without the solid, specific data yielded by research in descriptive and applied translation studies, while on the other hand one cannot even begin to work in one of the other two fields without having at least an intuitive theoretical hypothesis as one's starting point. In view of this dialectical relationship, it follows that, though the needs of a given moment may vary, attention to all three branches is required if the discipline is to grow and flourish.

3.32

The second point is that, in each of the three branches of translation studies, there are two further dimensions that I have not mentioned, dimensions having to do with the study, not of translating and translations, but of translation studies itself. One of these dimensions is historical: there is a field of the history of translation theory, in which some valuable work has been done, but also one of the history of translation description and of applied translation studies (largely a history of translation teaching and translator training) both of which are fairly well virgin territory. Likewise there is a dimension that might be called the methodological or meta-theoretical, concerning itself with problems of what methods and models can best be used in research in the various branches of the discipline (how translation theories, for instance, can be formed for greatest validity, or what analytic methods can best be used to achieve the most objective and meaningful descriptive results), but also devoting its attention to such basic issues as what the discipline itself comprises.

This paper has made a few excursions into the first of these two dimensions, but all in all it is meant to be a contribution to the second. It does not ask above all for agreement. Translation studies has reached a stage where it is time to examine the subject itself. Let the meta-discussion begin.

Notes

1. Written in August 1972, this paper is presented in its second pre-publication form with only a few stylistic revisions. Despite the intervening years, most of my remarks can, I believe, stand as they were formulated, though in one or two places I would phrase matters somewhat differently if I were writing today. In section 3.1224, for instance, subsequent developments in textual linguistics, particularly in Germany, are noteworthy. More directly relevant, the dearth of meta-reflection on the nature of translation studies, referred to at the beginning of section 3, is somewhat less striking today that in 1972, again thanks largely to German scholars. Particularly relevant is Wolfram Wilss' as yet unpublished paper "Methodische Probleme der allgemeinen und angewandten Übersetzungswissenschaft", read at a collloquium on translation studies held in Germersheim, West Gemany, 3-4 May 1975.
2. Michael Mulkay, "Cultural Growth in Science", in Barry Barnes (ed.), *Sociology of Science: Selected Readings* (Harmondsworth, Middlesex: Penguin; Modern Sociology Readings), pp. 126-141 (abridged reprint of "Some Aspects of Cultural Growth in the Natural Sciences", *Social Research*, 36 [1969], No. 1), quotation p. 136.
3. See e.g. W.O. Hagstrom, "The Differentiation of Disciplines", in Barnes, pp.

121-125 (reprinted from Hagstrom, *The Scientific Community* [New York: Basic Books, 1965], pp. 222-226).

4. Hagstrom, p. 123.

5. Here and throughout, these terms are used only in the strict sense of interlingual translating and translation. On the three types of translation in the broader sense of the word, intralingual, interlingual, and intersemiotic, see Roman Jakobson, "On Linguistic Aspects of Translation", in Reuben A. Brower (ed.), *On Translation* (Cambridge, Mass.: Harvard University Press, 1959), pp. 232-239.

6. Roger Goffin, "Pour une formation universitaire 'sui generis' du traducteur: Réflexions sur certain aspects méthodologiques et sur la recherche scientifique dans le domaine de la traduction", *Meta*, 16 (1971), 57-68, see esp. p. 59.

7. See the Hagstrom quotation in section 1.1. above.

8. Though, given the lack of a general paradigm, scholars frequently tend to restrict the meaning of the term to only a part of the discipline. Often, in fact, it would seem to be more or less synonymous with "translation theory".

9. Eugene Nida, *Towards a Theory of Translating, with Special Reference to Principles and Procedures Involved in Bible Translating* (Leiden: Brill, 1964).

10. Cf. Nida's later enlightening remark on his use of the term: "the science of translation (or, perhaps more accurately stated, the scientific *description* of the *processes* involved in translating)", Eugene A. Nida, "Science of Translation", *Language*, 45 [1969], 483-498, quotation p. 483 n. 1; my italics).

11. K.-Richard Bausch, Josef Klegraf, and Wolfram Wilss, *The Science of Translation: An Analytical Bibliography* (Tübingen: Tübinger Beiträge zur Linguistik). Vol. I (1970; TBL, No. 21) covers the years 1962-1969; Vol. II (1972; TBL, No. 33) the years 1970-1971 plus a supplement over the years covered by the first volume.

12. Werner Koller, "Übersetzen, Übersetzung und Übersetzer. Zu schwedischen Symposien über Probleme der Übersetzung", *Babel*, 17 (1971), 3-11, quotation p. 4. See further in this article (also p. 4) the summary of a paper "Übersetzungspraxis, Übersetzungstheorie und Übersetzungswissenschaft" presented by Koller at the Second Swedish-German Translators' Symposium, held in Stockholm, 23-24 October 1969.

13. Carl G. Hempel, *Fundamentals of Concept Formation in Empirical Science* (Chicago: University of Chicago Press, 1967; International Encyclopedia of Social Science, Foundations of the Unity of Sciences, II, Fasc. 7), p. 1.

14. I.A. Richards, "Toward a Theory of Translating", in Arthur F. Wright (ed.), *Studies in Chinese Thought* (Chicago: University of Chicago Press, 1953; also published as *Memoirs of the American Anthropological Association*, 55 [1953], Memoir 75), pp. 247-262.

15. Bacon's distinction was actually not between two types of research in the broader sense, but of experiments: "Experiments of Use" as against "Experiments of Light". See S. Pit Corder, "Problems and Solutions in Applied Linguistics", paper presented in a plenary session of the 1972 Copenhagen Congress of Applied Linguistics.

"Describing Literary Translations: Models and Methods" is the revised text of a paper presented at the International Colloquium on Literature and Translation held in Leuven, 27-29 April 1976. It was first published in James S Holmes, José Lambert, & Raymond van den Broeck (eds.), *Literature and Translation: New Perspectives in Literary Studies* (Leuven: Acco, 1978), pp. 69-82.

Describing Literary Translations: Models and Methods[1]

1. No one with an interest in translation studies, on looking through any standard bibliography of literary research, can fail to be struck by the fact that, of all the diligence and midnight oil represented in its listings, such a slight amount was spent on the examination of translations. For all their prime importance in the history of European literature, translations have by and large been ignored as bastard brats beneath the recognition (let alone concern) of truly serious literary scholars.

Even so, over the past century there have been what must sum up to hundreds of scholars who (to change the image) have moved out into what they considered the marches and outlying regions of literary studies, producing monographs that attempted, in one way or another, to describe the relations between a literary text or set of texts and its or their translation or translations. The appalling thing, really is not that there are, comparatively, so few such studies, but that so many of the studies that have been made are so haphazard, so piecemeal, so normative. And so naïve in their methodology.

The naïveté in particular is striking. All too frequently one closes a study of this kind with the feeling that its author, engrossed in his texts, failed to take time out to consider just what the process is that manifested itself between the existing original text and the new text produced by the translator. True, it is very useful to make a distinction between the product-oriented study of translations and the process-oriented study of translating. But this distinction cannot give the scholar leave to ignore the self-evident fact that the one is the result of the other, and that the nature of the product cannot be understood without a comprehension of the nature of the process.

During the past quarter century, of course, scholars have also devoted a great deal of thinking, if not of research, to the translation process as such. For the most part, these have been scholars of another ilk, not philologians but, primarily, linguists, now and then with the aid of a mathematician or psychologist. Yet the results of their thinking, too, would seem to be in large part simplistic and naïve, at least when applied to highly complex entities of the kind that "literary texts"[2] tend to be.

My point, then, is that if the emerging generation of scholars working with translations are to avoid the errors of their intellectual forebears, they must develop an adequate model of the translation process before they can hope to develop relevant methods for the description of translation products.

2.1. The earliest explicit, more or less formalized models of the translation process were designed in the late forties and early fifties as bases for programs of research into the feasibility of so-called automatic translation. These models started from the notion that texts were strings of words (or "lexical items") which could, in the main, be translated item by item, if only a few allowances were made for the unfortunate tendency of languages to exhibit language-pair differences in syntax and to create divergent exocentric (that is, "idiomatic") phrases.[3] Later this basically lexical-rank model was replaced by a sentence-rank model, in which (to cite the terminology used by one of its foremost advocates, Nida) a source-language passage was converted into a receptor-language passage via a tripartite process of analysis, kernel-level transfer, and restructuring.[4]

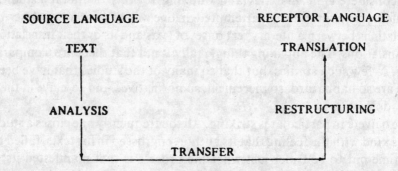

Figure 1. Nida's model of the translation process (Nida 1969:484).

The shift from lexical rank to sentence rank was a significant step towards sophistication, but the basic premise remained that a text is a string of units, essentially serial in nature.

2.2. A fundamental fact about texts, however, is that they are both serial *and* structural — that after one has read a text in time, one retains an array of data about it in an instantaneous form. On these grounds, it has more recently been suggested (though nowhere, as far as I know, clearly set out in model form) that the translation of texts (or at least of extensive texts, or at least of complex texts) takes place on two planes: a serial plane, where one translates sentence by sentence, and a structural plane, on which one abstracts a "mental conception" of the original text, then uses that mental conception as a kind of general criterion against which to test each sentence during the formulation of the new, translated text. This model might be sketched as follows:

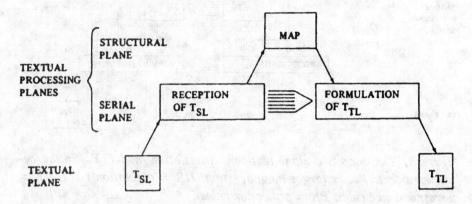

Figure 2. *Two-plane text-rank translation model (T_{SL} = source-language text; T_{TL} = target-language text).*

Such a two-plane model would seem to come much closer than the earlier serial models to describing the translation process as it takes place in the translator's study. The introduction of an abstract text-rank[5] "mental conception" — or, as I propose to call it henceforward, "map" — would seem to be a further step forward.

2.3. I would question, however, whether one such map or mental conception is sufficient to model the actual translation process adequately. Consider for a moment. Mr. X, who sometimes translates poetry into English, has just reread a poem in French, say Baudelaire's "La géante". Among the details in the map which he abstracts from the original poem will be (to restrict myself to a few of the more elementary features) that it is in sonnet form, rhyming *abba abba cde cde*, in syllabic verse, twelve (or thirteen) syllables to the line. X, if he is like most English-language translators, will not automatically decide to "retain" the rhyme scheme, the syllabic verse, or the twelve- (or thirteen-) syllable lines. Rather, he has a number of options to select from. On the basis of these selections (and a great many others) he in fact develops a second map, in various ways like the first, but in others quite different. It is this second map, not the first, which he uses as his criterion to guide him in carrying out his translation on the serial plane. If this really approximates the way in which the translator works, then we arrive at the following two-plane, two-map model:[6]

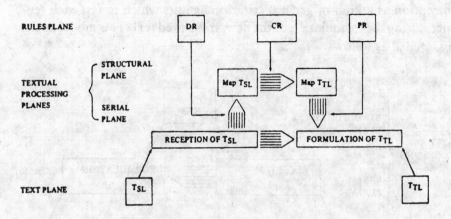

Figure 3. Two-map two-plane text-rank translation model (T_{SL} = source-language text; T_{TL} = target-language text; DR = derivation rules; CR = correspondence rules; PR = projection rules).

In my sketch of this model I have taken the further step of introducing three sets of rules by which specific phases of the translation process would seem to be carried out. (It goes without saying that in actual practice the different phases are not always separated from each other in time; like other human beings, the translator can be doing various things at once.[7]) Of the three rule sets, the first, that of derivation rules (DR), determines the way in which the translator abstracts his map of the source text from the text itself, and the third, that of projection rules (PR), determines the way in which he makes use of his map of the prospective target text in order to formulate the text, while the second, that of correspondence rules (CR) or matching rules (MR) — or, if one prefers, equivalence rules (ER) — determines the way in which he develops his target-text map from his source-text map. It should be noted that the first of the three phases described here the translator shares with every reader of literary texts, the third with every writer; the second, however, that of developing a target-text map from his source-text map by means of correspondence rules, is uniquely a translational (or least a specific kind of metatextual) operation, and as such deserves our special attention.

2.3.1. It should be realized in this connection that the map of the source text, if the translator-to-be who abstracts it is a skilled and experienced reader, will be a conglomerate of highly disparate bits of information. In the first place, as a map of a linguistic artefact, it will contain information, at a variety of ranks, regarding features of the text in its relation to the linguistic continuum within which (or violating the rules of which) it is formulated, that is, contextual information. Secondly, as a map of a literary artefact, it will contain information, at a variety of ranks, regarding features of the text in its relation to the literary continuum within which (or rebelling against which) it is formulated, that is, intertextual information. And third, as a map of a socio-cultural artefact, it will contain information, at a variety of ranks, regarding features of the text in its relation to the socio-cultural continuum within which (or transcending which) it is formulated, that is, situational information.[8]

2.3.2. In the case of all three types of information, and at the various ranks within each type, the translator, as soon as he sets about seeking correspondences with which to design his target-text map (or, in more everyday terms, as soon as he starts thinking "How am I going to translate this?"), is confronted by two dilemmas.

The first is that, for each feature in his source-text map, at least two kinds of corresponding target-text map features will usually be available. There will frequently be a feature which corresponds in form, but not in function — a feature which might therefore be called (if one may borrow the term from the biologists) a homologue. There will usually be a feature which corresponds in function, but not in form — an analogue. And there may also be a feature which corresponds in meaning, but in neither function nor form — should we, without the help of the biologists, call this a semantologue or semasiologue? It is a rare thing when the three happen to coincide across language barriers.

To return to my hypothetical translator Mr. X. Should he, in his English translation of "La géante", "retain" such features as syllabic verse, the twelve- and thirteen-syllable line, the "Continental" rhyme scheme, all of them homologues, that is to say, in the English setting parallel in form to the French, but clearly not in function? Or should he choose analogues: syllabotonic verse, ten-syllable lines, the rhyme scheme of the English sonnet? These are obviously momentous choices, and which ones he is to make and which to reject will be determined by the correspondence rules which the translator has consciously or unconsciously established on the basis of his confrontative knowledge of the French and English languages, literatures, and cultures. It is clear that his choices will not always be of the same kind for every type of information, or at every rank. For instance, translators usually choose homologues when dealing with socio-cultural features, but tend to choose analogues for many linguistic features, while they would seem to exercise a great deal of freedom of choice as regards the various features of poetic form: one finds accepted (and, I should think, acceptable) English translations that are formally homological, analogical, or a mixture of the two — and, indeed, many translations that have abandoned all correspondence in this regard.

That last remark points to the second dilemma. The experienced translator will have discovered that there is a certain interdependence among correspondences: the choice of a specific kind of correspondence in connection with one feature of the source-text map determines the kind of correspondence available for another or others, indeed in some cases renders correspondence for certain further features infeasible or even unattainable. The choice of blank verse instead of the rhymed couplet, for instance, confounds correspondence at the phonic level and makes correspondence on the end-stop/enjambment axis for all practical purposes impossible.

It follows that the translator, whether or not he is conscious of it, establishes a *hierarchy* of correspondences. Mr. X, for instance, may give priority to homological correspondence at the rank of "Continental" sonnet form, and as a result of this strict formal choice be compelled to reduce his correspondence requirements in regard to the semantic content of the poem. Or he may assign close matching of the semantic content such priority that he is forced to abandon any attempt at correspondence at the rank of sonnet form (perhaps justifying himself in doing so by arguing that free verse is a contemporary English analogue of the nineteenth-century French sonnet).

In the case of many less complex text types, of course, solutions to this problem of correspondence hierarchy are fairly clear. The translator of what (using for the moment a typology derived from the one developed by the Czech structuralists)[9] we may call an informative (or referential) text will tend to give full priority to semantic correspondence, and will retain other correspondences only when they do not interfere with that priority. In the case of a vocative (appellative, conative) text, for instance a TV commercial or a sermon, on the other hand, the translator (unless skewing of function is required) will give priority to establishing correspondence of appeal, even at the cost of having to overhaul the semantic message completely. The literary text, however — and whatever we may call its basic function: "poetic", "esthetic", "reflexive", "fictive" — is a much more complex entity, which may at various points (or indeed simultaneously) be informative, vocative, expressive, or for that matter meta-lingual or meta-literary. This makes the establishment of a hierarchy of correspondence priorities a much less clear-cut problem, and various translators will choose various solutions, none of which is demonstrably "right" or "wrong" (though the translator may think they are), but usually "somewhere in between".

3. If this is a fair description of the literary translation process, in other

words of the way in which the literary translator goes about his business, then the task for the scholar who wishes to describe the relationship between the translated text and its original would seem to be obvious. He must attempt to determine the features of the translator's two maps and to discover his three systems of rules, those of derivation, projection, and, above all, correspondence — in other words, the translator's poetics.

3.1. That is much more easily said than done, and I should like to devote some time to considering this problem further. In a few instances the analyst's task may be made somewhat less difficult for him. In the case of contemporary translations, for example, he may be able to consult the translator himself. But many translators, even brilliant ones, are less than eloquent in speaking or writing about their craft, and in any regard there is often a marked discrepancy between the explicit poetics a translator avows to subscribe to and the implicit, often subconscious poetics he adheres to in actual practice. Even in the case of older translations, there may be at least some pointers towards a poetics to be found in the translator's prefaces, commentaries, notes, letters, and the like. And the limits within which an individual poetics moves in a given literature in a given period can be demarcated *grosso modo* by a study of the translation theory of that literature in that period. Though in these instances, too, one must constantly be on the lookout for discrepancies between theory and practice.

3.2. In most cases, however, the analyst is left with little or no material beyond the two (or more) texts, the original and its translation(s), and it is. from these alone that he must attempt to derive his description. How can he set about his task? At the risk of simplifying the problem, I should like to restrict myself here to considering what I have suggested is the major aspect of this task, that of attempting to retrace the translator's two maps and the correspondence rules determining their relationship.

Clearly, the analyst will have to approach this problem in a different way from that of the translator. The translator, I have argued, derives a map of the source text from the text itself, next applies a set of correspondence rules, some of them more or less predetermined and some more or less *ad hoc*, to develop a target-text map from the source-text map, and finally uses this second map as a guide while formulating his target text. The analyst, on the other hand, starting from the two texts, will as a first step apply a set of derivation rules to each text in turn, in order to obtain maps of the two texts. His next step will be, with the aid of a set of comparison rules, to compare the two maps in order to determine the network ofcorrespondences between their various features. This will then be followed by a third

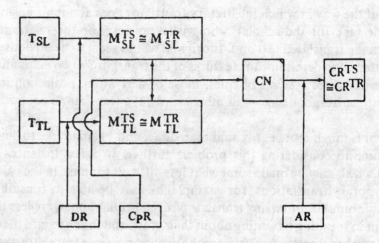

Figure 4. Model of the translation-descriptive process (T = text; SL = source language; TL = target language; M = map; TR = translator; TS = translation scholar; CN = network of correspondences; CR = correspondence rules; DR = derivation rules; CpR = comparison rules; AR = abstraction rules).

step in which, with the aid of a set of abstraction rules, he derives a set of correspondence rules and a correspondence hierarchy from the network of correspondences.

Only in one phase of one of these steps does the work of the analyst parallel that of the translator: in the operation of deriving the source-text map from the text. The operation of deriving the target-text map, on the other hand, is for the analyst the reverse of the operation performed by the translator (though at the same time parallel to the analyst's operation of deriving the source-text map, and requiring comparable discovery procedures). Similarly, the abstraction of a network of correspondences from the maps, and of correspondence rules and a correspondence hierarchy underlying that network, is an operation of quite a different kind from those performed by the translator.

A further complication is one that applies to all studies of mental processes. Since in most cases there is little or no tangible evidence of what has taken place in the translator's "mind" except the text he has produced as compared to the original text, the scholar attempting to trace the relationship of the two texts likewise in most cases has no material except those two texts from which to derive his conclusions. And since the descriptive process he pursues is, though in a different way from the translator's process, extremely complex, there is great danger that the results of his analysis will be highly subjective and so of little value to other scholars. Assuming that objectivity in any true sense is in such a matter a goal even more unattainable than in research dealing with tangible objects and/or events observable outside the "mind", one can nevertheless posit that a high degree of intersubjectivity is an aim worth striving after in a research situation of this kind.

3.3. There would seem to be a choice for the analyst between two basic working methods. In the first, the descriptive scholar, upon studying the two texts, will derive from them a list of distinctive features which strike him as significant and deserving of comparative analysis; frequently he will also determine a hierarchical ordering of the features. The well-trained analyst will, it must be assumed, bring with him a detailed knowledge of linguistic, literary, and socio-cultural theory such that he can identify contextual, intertextual, and situational elements in the texts in a manner acceptable to other scholars, and this, it must likewise be assumed, will provide at least a modicum of intersubjectivity to his application of linguistic, literary, and socio-cultural research methods. But the fact remains that none of the disciplines concerned with the nature of texts has given us a generally accepted intersubjective method for determining distinctive features in a concrete text, so that their selection remains to a large extent an *ad hoc* operation. The result will consequently be that the maps of the two texts derived by the analyst, like the translator's two maps, will be incomplete: the analyst, for instance, may very likely discover blank spaces (indications of *terrae incognitae*) in the translator's maps, but overlook the blank spaces in his own — and precisely in such *terrae incognitae*, as in parts of Africa in the old maps, may be lions.

A second working method, at least in theory, would be to circumvent the problem of *ad hoc* selection of distinctive features by determining beforehand a required repertory of features always to be analysed, regardless of what specific text is involved. This method, too, has at least one major drawback: if its results are to lead to a map that is generally acceptable as within reach of completeness, the repertory would have to be quite extensive, and the task of providing full details on the texts would be one that is arduous and tedious to the researcher and largely uninteresting to the reader.

The repertory method would, however, assure a higher degree of intersubjectivity to the results of the analysis based on it — provided, of course, that scholars in the field could reach agreement as to what elements should be included in such a repertory. Lambert has made an explorative attempt at a listing;[10] it would seem to me that a further filling out and structuring of this listing should be one of the major foci of research and discussion in the near future for scholars interested in translation description. It is clear that the repertory must not only be quite complete, but also complex enough in structure to accommodate a number of parametric axes. Among these a major one, of course, is the axis microstructure-mesostructure-macrostructure (from grapheme/morpheme via lexeme, sentence, and suprasentential units to text; in verse moreover via line, stanza, and suprastanzaic units). But other axes intersect this one, notably that of form-meaning-function (morphologue-semasiologue-analogue) and that of (linguistic) contextuality - (literary) intertextuality - (socio-cultural) situationality, and these axes too would have to be incorporated.

The task of working out such a repertory would be enormous. But if scholars were to arrive at a consensus regarding it, in the way, for instance, that botanists since Linnaeus have arrived at a consensus regarding systematic methods for the description of plants, it would then become possible, for the first time, to provide descriptions of original and translated texts, of their respective maps, and of correspondence networks, rules, and hierarchies that would be mutually comparable. And only on the basis of mutually comparable descriptions can we go on to produce well-founded studies of a larger scope: comparative studies of the translations of one author or one translator, or — a greater leap — period, genre, one-language (or one-culture), or general translation histories.

Such goals, of course, the scholars of our generation have tended to reject: they seem to us unattainable, and so outside the range of our less-than-vaulting ambition. It is in any case certain that they exceed the grasp of the subjective, largely intuitive and impressionist methods still so often being applied today. And only a more explicit, a more precise, a stricter and more intersubjective approach holds any promise of greater things to come.

Notes

1. The part of this paper devoted to the model of the translation process is an outgrowth of a seminar on the subject held with students at the University of Amsterdam in the spring of 1975. This model also served as the theme for talks given at the University of Iowa in December 1975, at the International Comparative Literature Association's Colloquium on Translation Theory organized in Budapest on 18 and 19 August 1976, and at the State University of New York, Binghamton, in January 1977. Remarks made during discussion of the talks at Iowa City, Budapest, and Binghamton, as well as those brought forward at the Leuven colloquium, have led to clarification of points here and there in the first part of the paper.

2. I use the term here assuming that we are more or less agreed on the core of its meaning, and without attempting anything approaching a definition.

3. See e.g. the discussions in various early computer-oriented studies.

4. In the various models developed at this level, the main difference of opinion is in just what is being transferred: syntactic elements (Nida's kernel or near-kernel sentences) or semantic kernels. (Eugene A. Nida, "Science of Translation", *Language*, 45 [1969], pp. 483-498). The fullest discussion of these and other serial models of the translation process is to be found in V.N. Komissarov, *Slovo o perevode* (Moscow: IMO, 1973), a book which I am unfortunately unable to read, though manuscript translations of several portions of it made by various students at the University of Amsterdam have given me confidence that it is a work of high significance which needs to be translated into a Western language *in toto*.

5. Obviously, in the case of longer texts there will also be mesostructural ranks, ranging from those of paragraphs and/or stanzas to those of chapters of novels, cantos of long poems, scenes or acts of plays.

6. Of course the charge can be made that this model, too, is an oversimplification of the translation process, ignoring as it does the mesostructural ranks. Eventually it may therefore prove necessary to abandon it in favour of a more complex model introducing a hierarchical series of maps, ranging from sentence-rank maps via a number of mesostructural maps to the text maps.

7. It also goes without saying that there is a great deal of feedback not indicated in the model; details of the target-text map, and in some cases even of the source-text map, may change drastically in the course of sentence-by-sentence (or transeme-by-transeme) translation.

8. On this terminology see André Lefevere; "The Translation of Literature: An Approach", *Babel*, 16 (1970), pp. 75-79, and pp. 45-52 above.

9. And deriving originally from Bühler. Cf. e.g. Roman Jakobson, "Closing Statement: Linguistics and Poetics", Thomas A. Sebeok (ed.), *Style in Language* (Cambridge, Mass.: M.I.T. Press, 1960), pp. 350-377, esp. pp. 353-357.

10. José Lambert, "Echanges littéraires et traduction: Discussion d'un projet", James S Holmes, José Lambert, & Raymond van den Broeck (eds.), *Literature and Translation: New Perspectives in Literary Studies* (Leuven, Acco, 1978), pp. 142-160, esp. pp. 154-155.

"Translation Theory, Translation Theories, Translation Studies, and the Translator" was presented as a plenary address at the Eighth World Congress of the International Federation of Translators (FIT) held in Montreal, 12-18 May 1977, and published in the proceedings: Paul A. Horguelin (ed.), *Translating, A Profession* (Ottawa: Canadian Translators and Interpreters Council, 1978), pp. 55-61. A Dutch summary appeared in *Van Taal tot Taal* (Amsterdam), 21 (1977), No. 4, pp. 29-30.

Translation Theory, Translation Theories, Translation Studies, and the Translator

I am going to try to be brief and I hope that my briefness is not going to be the kind that Mr. Vinay, via Mr. Darbelnet, spoke of yesterday: when people say they are going to be brief they turn out to be longer than anyone else! One of the reasons for being brief is that when I got to Montreal I had a chance to read through Popovič's paper and I questioned whether I really needed to say anything; now that I have heard both Mr. Popovič's and Mr. Toper's papers, I am quite certain that there is not much need for me to say all that much more. Nevertheless, some remarks. This is the core of what would have been a longer paper if so many things had not already been said by the other speakers.

Before I begin, I have to confess that I do not read the Slavic languages and, as you can understand, this is a great handicap for anyone interested in translation theory. It means that the knowledge I have of Russian, Polish, and Czechoslovak translation theory is based either on personal conversations, or on articles that have appeared in translation, or, in a few cases, on abstracts that students of mine have made for me. On this point, I would like to take this opportunity to mention to the Russian representative that it would be a great deal of help to us in the West if they would consider providing abstracts in a Western language of the articles that they publish. There are a great many of us, I think, who are interested in problems of translation theory and translation studies who do not know Russian and who have a terribly frustrating feeling that there is a great deal going on that is inaccessible to us.

But this is only a side comment at the beginning. In my remarks, I want to place the main emphasis on how far we have got or have not got in translation theory, and where we should go from here. I will therefore perhaps be somewhat more negative about where we are than our two previous speakers. It has been mentioned that we have had translation theory for thousands of years now — I suppose we could start with Cicero — but this is theory in the very loose sense that any general statement or series of statements about a phenomenon is a sort of theory of that phenomenon. More strictly, we could define a theory as a series of statements, each of which is derived logically from a previous statement or from an axiom and which together have a strong power of explanation and prediction regarding a certain phenomenon. Now, until the day the FIT was founded, twenty-four years ago, it could not be argued that there had been any serious attempt in the West (I can't speak for Russia) at forming theory in the strict sense of the translation phenomenon. At about this time we begin to find a new kind of writing about translation — writing which often presented itself as a theory of translation. Nevertheless, most of the theoretical presentations that we have had until now, although they have called themselves theories, are not really theories in the strict sense. They have an air of unclear thinking about the problems before them without the strict logical development of a theory. At the same time, most of the theories we had before the fifties were clearly and undeniably normative. They told us how we *should* translate rather than how people *do* translate, and many of the theories we have had since that time have become implicitly normative theories while pretending to be non-normative theories. Even now, we continue to tell people how to translate although we set out to try to define what people are doing when they translate. Most theories that we have had in the twenty-four years since 1953 are in fact only partial theories as well as normative theories about the translation process or, in a few cases, about the translation product.

Here I have made a distinction which I will say more about. People who are in literary studies had in the past been primarily interested in looking at existing translations — translation products — and seeing what kind of texts they were. Linguists have been primarily interested in what takes place between the input sentence in one language and the output in the other language — what takes place starting from the original text and looking toward the result rather than starting from the result and looking back toward the original text. Linguistic theories, on the other hand, have the great advantage of working with a highly formalized language; of being able to provide models and to make use of standard forms of terminology. One of the great drawbacks of practically all the linguistic translation theories that we have had up to now has been that they have had to work with a linguistics which is only interested in the sentence and linguistic phenomena below the sentence level; linguistics itself in the structural period and even in the transformational period had been very frightened of going beyond the sentence. Translation on the other hand, and certainly literary translation, is so obviously a question not of translating a series of sentences but of translating a text which happens to consist of sentences among other things that the linguistic approach has had the great shortcoming in practically all the linguistic theories that I know of not being able to touch this aspect of translation: the text level.

The theories developed by the literary scholars on the other hand have the disadvantage that they, working within the literary tradition, have been far less formalized (the authors seemed almost frightened of any standard terminology) yet, on the other hand, they have had the advantage of looking at texts as texts and not merely as a serial continuation of sentences. My criticism of the theories of literary scholars at this time should be somewhat less strong. The recent development, especially in Northwestern Europe, West Germany, and the Low Countries, of text studies as a discipline opens new vistas for the literary study of texts. In the future it will, I should think, be of great value to those trying to develop theories of translation at the text level. Up to now, there has been far too little use made of this new text-studies approach in studying translations.

I have mentioned the distinction between theories which look at the translation process and those which look at the translation product; there is a third point which I might introduce here. A whole area of study has hardly been touched upon — and that is the area of the translation function: how a translated text functions in the society into which it comes. This "translation sociology", as you might call it, is an area where the theorists have not really given us much to work on yet. No one, at least to my knowledge, at least in the West, has yet even dared to face up to the need for a "field theory" of the entire range of the translation phenomenon. Such a field theory would be built up of a number of partial theories and it would seem to me that we would need at least four such theories. We need a theory of the translation *process*, that is, the theory of what happens when people decide to translate something. We need a theory of the translation *product*, that is to say, what is specific to the translated text as a text; in what ways is it similar to and in what ways is it different from other kinds of texts, literary or other. We need a theory of the translation *function*, that is, how the translation works in the recipient society. And we need a theory of translation *didactics*. The first three of these partial theories, I feel, should be non-normative. They should be attempts to provide models by which we could analyse existing situations, describing not what the situation should be but what it is. The fourth, on the other hand, the theory of translation didactics, is necessarily normative. We have to make decisions about how to train translators whether we know the answers or not, simply because translators have to be trained. It seems to me, in fact, that many of the theories of translation that we have had up to now, while pretending to be theories of the translation process, are in fact theories for translation didactics. They are giving us material to train translators. Now, I wonder whether we can really develop a good theory of translation didactics before we spend more energy on developing the three non-normative translation theories I mentioned. It seems to me that before we can know how to train translators, we have to know what takes place in the translation process and we have to know what translated texts are.

Another point I would make is that much of our theorizing seems to have been armchair theorizing without experimenting in controlled situations to find out what actually happens. As for the theory of the translation process for instance, abandoning the sentence-level approach of earlier theorists, various theorists over the last ten years have proposed a more complex model of the translation process. Levý, for instance, suggested using the terminology of game theory and suggested that the translator has an overall strategy for winning the game of translation; from this overall strategy we develop tactics for the solution of individual problems at the sentence or paragraph or chapter level. Toury, the Tel Aviv scholar, has developed a structuration of norms — the translator begins with certain primary norms and other secondary norms, and this hierarchy varies for individuals. I have suggested that actually the translation process is a multi-level process; while we are translating sentences, we have a map of the original text in our minds and at the same time a map of the kind of text we want to produce in the target language. Even as we translate serially, we have this structural concept so that each sentence in our translation is determined not only by the sentence in the original but by the two maps of the original text and of the translated text which we are carrying along as we translate.

Now, these three theories, which differ from each other more in terminology than in actual approach, all emphasize the fact that there is a text approach and a sentence approach and that these two have to be brought into harmony with each other. To find out more about how these models work, we should have a large body of controlled experimentation with actual translators to come to a more careful delineation of the translation process. Up to now, this has hardly been done.

Another example comes to mind. I have often read that the translation should have the same level of reading ease as the original text. That is a normative concept. You can state it hypothetically: there is a hypothesis that a translation should have the same level of reading ease as the original. Let us assume that we are going to test this hypothesis. I did this last year with eight English novels and their Dutch translations and eight Dutch novels and their English translations, tested with a group of students. It turned out that the eight English novels became somewhat more difficult to read when translated into Dutch. That would be a natural result when one considers the amount of extra information one has to build into a translation. But the eight Dutch novels translated into English gave different results: four of them were easier to read in English translation according to the testees while the other four became much more difficult.

This demonstrates that there are other factors at work in the translator's strategy in addition to "reading ease" and that, at least for these translations from Dutch into English, one cannot conclude that the translators used reading ease as a norm.

This kind of experimentation is something we need a great deal more of and I do not believe that we can get much further in translation theory until we have had many more attempts at translation experiment, description, and research with concrete material. Research not in the traditional literary sense but in controlled situations where one states a certain hypothesis and sets out to test it using the methods of the social sciences.

I believe that these were the two main things that I was planning to say which have not been said in quite the same way by the other two speakers. I would like to say just a little bit, then, about the relevance of this whole area, translation theory, translation theories, and translation studies, to the translator. Translation scholars are constantly being confronted by translators with the questions: What's the use of what's being done? What does it do to help me? First of all, I would like to question whether helping the translator is really a criterion for translation studies. Mr. Osers said the other night that one can study a great deal of art history without becoming a better artist for it, or one can study a great deal of musicology without becoming a better musician or composer. It need not be a main aim of translation studies to help the translator. But can they be of help to translators? The value that a translation theory has for its practitioners in general depends on the state of the theory, and there are theories and disciplines which are of great value to their practitioners because they have been so highly developed that they provide a great deal of insight into the phenomenon. Other theories are still insufficiently developed to provide that insight. I'm afraid that, taken all in all and by comparison with very many other disciplines, the state of translation theory is still not very powerful in the sense that it does not explain the phenomena to the extent that we should like it to. I hope that before long it will be more powerful than it is now, but even in its present state, translation theory can, I believe, be a great deal of help, on a general level, to translators. I don't know whether there are any biologists present to back me up on this, but I have read that the bumble-bee should not be able to fly because its body is too heavy for its wing span. The bumble-bee doesn't know this and so it flies. For centuries, translators have been "flying like bumble-bees", not realizing that they can't, that it is an impossibility that they have tackled. Reading translation theory and thinking about translation problems, one reaches a dead point when one feels blocked in every direction and can't do anything; such is the frustration about the whole situation that one thinks about giving up translation. At that point, translation theory can do a great deal to help make us aware of a great many more things to help us over that dead point so that, from that point on, we could translate much more consciously, being much more aware of the choices. We can get rid of some of the almost childlike beliefs that we have worked with for a long time (it has to be done this way, this way is always wrong, this way is always right) and realize that in this situation, *this* is perhaps the most appropriate tactic and in that situation, *that* is perhaps the most appropriate tactic. If translation theory, even at its present state, can give us some more awareness of what we are doing as translators and help us to think and become conscious of our activity, then I think it has fulfilled an important role. Nevertheless, I hope that at, let's say, two conferences from now, we will be able to tell you at FIT that translation theory in the West is six years or seven years further on and that we have accomplished wonderful things in the meantime.

"The Future of Translation Theory: A Handful of Theses" was presented as a paper at the International Symposium on Achievements in the Theory of Translation held in Moscow and Yerevan, 23-30 October 1978, under the auspices of the Literary Translation Council of the Soviet Writers' Union. A Dutch translation entitled "De toekomst van de vertaaltheorie: Een handvol stellingen" was published in André Lefevere & Ria Vanderauwera (eds.), *Literatuur, vertaalwetenschap, vertaling en vertalen* (Leuven: Acco, 1979; special issue of the Belgian review *Restant*, 7 [1978-1979], No. 4), pp. 245-249.

The Future of Translation Theory: A Handful of Theses

This is not the traditional kind of cogently reasoned academic paper. Instead, it is a series of theses about the theory of translation — theses which I shall not attempt to prove, but which I posit in the belief that they are not merely hypotheses, but demonstrable truths.

They are based on my reading in traditional and modern translation theory and my ruminations on the state of the art. Over the years, this reading has been quite extensive — and intensive. There is, however, at least one major lacuna in it. Since I do not know Russian, I have read only that small tip of the vast Soviet translation-theory iceberg that juts above the surface of Western thinking by having been translated. Far too little *has* been translated, far too much has *not*, and hence the work of a great many theorists, from Čukovskij via Revzin and Rozencvejg to Koptilov and Komissarov (to mention but a few), remains for me little more than hearsay. The consequence is that some of these theses that I posit as true may be true only for the situation in the West, and not (or no longer) for that in the Soviet Union. If so, I apologize for my ignorance.

1

One of the major obstacles to the development of a sound and comprehensive general theory of translation has been the inability of scholars in various fields to communicate with each other. Linguists and literary scholars speak very different academic dialects, and most of either type of scholar would seem unable to move outside their own discipline, with its specific norms, codes, concerns, and rigours, far enough to be able to "translate" and integrate what scholars in the other discipline are saying. Nor have they been able to "translate" and integrate the everyday-speech statements of practising translators about their translation activity.

2

Traditionally, it was primarily literary scholars, together with a few stray theologians, who turned their minds to the formulation of general notions about the nature of translation and translations. They all too often erred in mistaking their personal, national, or period norms for general translation laws. Andthey all too frequently substituted impressionism for methodology. Seen in retrospect, their saving grace is that they were, almost always, aware that they were dealing with *texts*, and that translations of those texts must themselves in all but exceptional cases function as texts.

3

Work in the field of translation theory over the past twenty-five years has been done primarily by linguists, theoretical or applied. They have, by and large, moved down a different road, one that has turned out to be a dead end. Accepting the basic self-imposed restrictions of structural and/or transformational linguistics, they have devoted their energies to the problem of how to find what they have labelled "equivalent" target-language glosses for source-language words, groups of words, and/or (at best) sentences considered out of context.

4

Glossing at this micro-structural level constitutes only a lesser part of the translator's activity in producing functional target-language texts. The rendering of a source-language text into a target language as a series of sentences in isolation does not lead to a translation in any true sense of the term.

5

No adequate general theory of translation can be developed before scholars have turned from a sentence-restricted linguistics to produce a full theory of the nature of texts. Such a theory will devote extensive attention to the *form* of texts — how their parts work together to constitute an entity —, to the way texts convey often very complex patterns of *meaning*, and to the manner in which they *function* communicatively in a given socio-cultural setting.

6

Traditional translation theorists often defined the relation between an original text and a translated text derived from it as one of identity: a translation, or at least a "good" translation, was, or should be, "the same as" its original. When this position was seen to be untenable, it was replaced by the notion that the relation is one of "equivalence", and "equivalence" and "equivalent" are key terms in almost all recent theoretical works. (Synonymy, also a highly debatable term in this context, is something of a competitor.) Equivalence is quite likely the goal of painstaking translators. But it is a goal that always exceeds their grasp.

What the translator actually achieves is not textual *equivalence* in any strict sense of the term, but a network of *correspondences*, or *matchings*, with a varying closeness of *fit*. These correspondences are of various kinds, formal, semantic, and/or functional, mimetic, or analogical, and achieved at various levels of the translated text, micro-, meso-, and/or macrostructural. Defining the nature of these correspondences and minimum and maximum degrees of fit should be a major task of the translation theorist.

7
Definitions of translation which postulate only correspondence in meaning as essential (semantic-correspondence definitions) are not valid definitions, since demonstrably not all texts generally accepted as translations conform to such a requirement. The same holds true for definitions postulating only correspondence in function (pragmatic-correspondence definitions), or for that matter correspondence in form (syntactic-correspondence definitions). Such definitions are in reality no more than codifications of time, place, and/or text-type-bound norms of an individual or a smaller or larger group, mistakenly elevated to the position of universal translation laws.

8
Many of the weaknesses and naïvetés of contemporary translation theories are a result of the fact that the theories were, by and large, developed deductively, without recourse to actual translated texts-in-function, or at best to a very restricted corpus introduced for illustration rather than for verification or falsification. If and when we ever do arrive at a comprehensive translation theory which meets the rigorous requirements of a true scientific theory explaining the nature of *all* the phenomena to be considered, that theory — for all science's desire for the elegance of simplicity — will be much more complex than any that has been presented up to now, since it will have to account for a great many variables which usually either are assumed to be constants (see the preceding thesis) or are ignored entirely.

9
Such a comprehensive theory of translation cannot be produced by armchair rumination in splendid isolation. It will have to be the product of teamwork between specialists in a variety of fields — text studies, linguistics (particularly psycho- and socio-linguistics), literary studies, psychology, and sociology. *And* with the involvement of practising translators. It will have to be based on analyses of a great many translated texts of various kinds, from a variety of times and places, written in many languages, and functioning in a diversity of cultures. A second need is —

something which has hardly been done at all up to now — the involvement of practising translators in an extensive series of laboratory-type investigations into the ways in which translators actually work.

10

Let me give an illustration of the value of involving practising translators in research of this kind. Theorists, though most of them are not very clear on this point, tend to present the translation process as a serial process, a process moving in time from the first sentence of a text to the last. In-depth interviews that are being conducted with practising translators in Amsterdam and elsewhere indicate that this is not usually the case. True, the actual act of putting a translation to paper (or at least the first draft of it) is to a large extent serial. But this serial process appears to be governed, at least in most cases, by another process that is structural in nature: that of, in the first place, abstracting from the source text its structure as a textual entity, analysing the interrelationships of the various parts in this structure, and defining the way in which this entity functions (or functioned in the past) in its socio-cultural setting — this followed by, in the second place, defining the structure of the translated text-to-be, the relation of its parts to the whole, and the function it is to have in its new socio-cultural situation. To consider a translation solely as a serial process, ignoring this second, governing structural plane, can only lead to a theory so oversimplified as to be useless.[1]

11

A further prerequisite for the development of a full-blown general theory of translation is that we each need to know more about what the other is doing. And now I am not referring primarily to the "translation" failure across disciplines, but to the barriers to knowledge across national and linguistic frontiers. There is a crying need for a better, more systematic method of international dissemination of information regarding research in the field. The annual bibliographies in *Masterstvo perevoda*, international in scope, are highly to be praised in this regard. It is unfortunate that, given the limited knowledge of Russian in the West, so much of the knowledge listed in them remains a closed book to so many of us. I do not believe that I am speaking only for myself when I say that in the West one of the most urgent needs, if we are to come closer to the kind of translation theory I have outlined, is for rapid, reliable, and extensive information, via translations and abstracts, on the vast amount of work that has been and is being done on translation theory in the Soviet Union.

1. For a model of the translation process developed from this perspective, see pp. 81-91 above.

The State of Two Arts: Literary Translation and Translation Studies in the West Today

In memory of Anton Popovič

Literary translation in the Western world today is a panorama of many shadows, brightened here and there by a ray of light. To paint that panorama in all its vast complexity would challenge the skills of a chiaroscuro master. To try one's hand at sketching it in a few brief paragraphs is a vain endeavour that only a fool would undertake. This is one fool's attempt.

The shadows are many, and I shall describe only a few that catch the eye. As it has ever been, or at least for centuries, the general public still tends to look upon translation as a quite simple matter, the substituting of a word for a word, a phrase for a phrase, with at most here and there a small linguistic adjustment because languages are after all somewhat idiosyncratic. The translator is, in this simplistic common-sense view, a kind of cross-linguistic transcriber or copyist, a slightly glorified typist. At best a craftsman, comparable perhaps to a carpenter or a housepainter.

And the literary translator is still reimbursed accordingly. He, or more often she, works hours per day, and days (or nights) per week, that seem to everyone else something out of Dickens' nineteenth century. She types and retypes her own manuscripts, since a typist costs more than she does, and a word processor is a far too expensive gadget to be anything but a dream. And for it all she earns less than a minimum wage, in actual buying power less than she would have earned ten or fifteen years ago.

Meanwhile the publishing situation has become an ever-deepening shadow. The major publishers, who once prided themselves on their

"The State of Two Arts: Literary Translation and Translation Studies in the West Today" is a paper presented at the Tenth World Congress of the International Federation of Translators (FIT) held in Vienna, 17-23 August 1984. It was first printed in the proceedings: Hildegund Bühler (ed.), *Translators and Their Position in Society* (Vienna: Braunmüller, 1985), pp. 147-153.

gentlemanly profession and their cultural responsibilities, have in many cases (and here the New York situation must be seen as the wave of the future) been swallowed up by larger corporate entities that believe books should be sold pretty much like soap. As a result, their activities are, by and large, focused increasingly on the best-seller and the trendy subject of the moment, and serious fiction, unless it has trendy best-seller qualities, is tending more and more to fall by the wayside, where poetry has long already lain.

With only rare exceptions (of which Umberto Eco's *Name of the Rose* is the current instance), translations, which are in any case more expensive to produce than books in the original, are notoriously not best-sellers in the dominant language areas — unless, again, they deal with a trendy subject: the Third World, for instance, Eastern European dissidence, the Holocaust... The result is that, compared to the fifties and sixties, less and less of the total production of major publishers in the dominant language areas consists of translations, and even those that do achieve publication are themselves almost always from another of those areas. To judge by what the New York publishers, for instance, are bringing out, we would seem to have moved into an Age of Literary Isolationism.

The shadows, I said, are deep. Yet there are also rays of light. The failure of major presses is more and more finding recompense in the activities of smaller, more daring, farther-ranging publishers. Here again, the American situation provides an indication of the way we would seem to be going, with university presses and small independent publishers taking over many of the tasks that used to be part of the New York publishers' normal activities, issuing novels from extremely strange places, more translated poetry than ever before, and a wide range of other texts that excel in quality rather than in prospective sales. Though it follows that, without either the renown or the promotion and distribution facilities of the major publishers, they have even less financial elbow-room to pay translators properly.

More significant, and perhaps the major highlight, is the fact that among that part of the public that is truly interested in things literary there is at last a growing sophistication in attitude about the nature of translation: an increasing awareness of the artistry involved in this process which is, in I.A. Richards' overquoted phrase, one of the most complex activities in the cosmos.

The recognition that literary translation at its best is a rare art form has in its turn led, if not to a higher level of income for the run-of-the-literary-mill translator, at least to a vastly increased recognition of the art in the shape of a proliferation of local, national, and international grants, awards, and prizes. In 1956, when I received the Dutch award for translation, the Martinus Nijhoff Prize, it was one of a child's handful of such awards in the entire world. This year, when I received its new counterpart in Flanders, the Prize of the Flemish Community for Literary Translation, it was merely one of the very many there are today.

At the same time, though critics throughout the Western world still tend on the whole to ignore the translatorial aspects of the translated books they are reviewing, or at most, if they are offended by the translation, to niggle over a "wrong" rendering of a word or phrase, there would appear to be a growing number of journals — a notable case is the *New York Review of Books* (for some good things, too, come from Gotham) — which deal at reflective length with translation quality and translation problems as themselves a subject of interest to the editors, the critics, and, presumably, the readers.

It is not a panorama, rather a vignette. But I must hurry on. Not only has literary translation received a certain degree (though a degree still far too small) of esteem among the literary public. It has also gradually attracted more attention, and attained greater respectability, as a legitimate subject for consideration, reflection, and research within academe. Translating, and working with translations, have both been part and parcel of the scholar's terrain for ages, but they were always considered as nothing more than tools in the service of some other, higher scholarly goal. Even twenty years ago, the university-based researcher who focused on translating or translations as phenomena deserving of his (or, all too rarely, her) unswerving attention as objects for research was generally deemed a wrong-headed if harmless eccentric.

Serious academic interest in translation problems on a larger scale first came, in the later fifties and the sixties, from the side of the applied linguists. This became especially visible in West Germany, where a sizable number of new translation schools had been created after the war, and a younger generation of scholars, confronted by a conglomeration of problems unheard of in their books of structuralist linguistics, dared to give those problems priority above academic respectability. Their efforts, at first hindered by the inhibitions of a training which looked on the Sapir-Whorf hypothesis as a linguistic axiom and hampered by the limitations in the methodology of linguistic structuralism, fared little better after the triumph of the more universalist approach of Chomsky and the transformationalists. For that school, too, clung long to the basic premise that, "at least for the time being", the upper limit for research in linguistics should be the sentence.

It was to take years before the awareness broke through that communication is not primarily a question of individual sentences, well-formed or not, but of texts or discourses, larger-scale units of communication functioning within contexts, intertexts, and situations that elude the analyst at sentence level and structured according to much more complex rules than the one of sentence strings. The emergence of discourse analysis in America and of *Textwissenschaft* on the European continent has pointed the way in more recent years for research into the nature of textual structuring and of the specific rules and conventions governing various kinds and types of texts. There are still too few tangible, usable results, and there is perhaps still too little diachronic research ("Is this a universal quality of this text type, or only one for this culture, at this time?"). But research would seem to be heading in the right direction for a better understanding of the fundamental problems of translating, which in their accidentals may manifest themselves at sentence level or below it, but in their essentials are surely suprasentential.

If for the linguist the problem involved in studying translational phenomena has been complicated by changes of paradigm within his or her discipline, for the literary scholar it has been magnified out of all proportions by the fact that there is not really a disciplinary paradigm at all, but rather a far-too-rapid succession of fashions and frills of the moment, from New Criticism to literary structuralism to literary sociology to post-structuralism to reception studies to deconstruction. The one thing that most (though by no means all) of these modish approaches have shared has been that the "literature" of a cultural area is a question of a corpus of texts that have been canonized, that is to say, accepted by the community as of high literary worth, and that the task of the literary scholar is to develop methods for the better understanding of texts in the canon. Looked at from this point of view, the currently fashionable approach to literary studies, deconstructionism, differs little from New Criticism, or for that matter from hermeneutics before it.

Inspected more closely, however, deconstructionism is marked by a major difference that could theoretically be of quite some value for translation studies. For the traditional interpretative approaches, a main aim of the literary scholar was to demonstrate that, despite all the paradoxes and contradictions apparent at the surface of a text, there was an underlying unity to it, which surface complexities demonstrably served to enhance. The deconstructionist's task, as he or she sees it, is quite a different kind of demonstrating. Beneath a surface unity, he seeks the contradictions and paradoxes which uncover the underlying motives, desires, and frustrations the author of the text has done his best to hide. This approach, with the techniques deconstructionism has developed to apply it, opens up two avenues (or possibly by-roads) of study in connection with literary translations. First of all, it has long been posited, most explicitly by Jiří Levý, that there is a tendency for translators to iron away disturbing irregularities in the texts they are translating. To what extent, then, do translators as a result smooth out precisely those disturbing contradictions which, the deconstructionists would have us believe, make the original text exciting? But translators are also human beings, despite all their efforts to function as clear-glass windows which the bright sun of the author's text can shine through undistorted. And that fact gives rise to a second question: To what extent are the texts that they have translated unwitting records of their own motives, desires, and frustrations? The questions are important, and the deconstructionists are providing us with tools to answer them. As long as their main concern remains focused squarely on the canon to the exclusion of translations, which almost by definition do not belong to the canon, it cannot be expected that they will search for such answers themselves.

Along with the dominant current within the discipline, of looking upon literary studies as focused on a canon and its interpretation, there has long been a counter-current more interested in the ways in which texts function within a literary culture: how they get written, published, and reviewed, how they get read or ignored, how (and when) they win a place in the canon ... and in most cases how they eventually lose it. This approach has the distinct advantage (for translation studies as for many other fields of interest) of casting its nets wide enough to include a vast variety of "lesser" texts ignored by the canonists, from translation to "popular" literature. At the same time, in its guise as literary sociology it has long suffered from the lack of a clear over-all conceptual framework to lend it coherence as an alternative.

Building on the groundwork of the Russian structuralists, and availing themselves of work on metatexts and the literary communication process done in Slovakia and the Low Countries, Itamar Even-Zohar and scholars grouped around him at Tel Aviv have in recent years provided us with such a conceptual framework in their ongoing definition of the fortunes of literary texts as a "polysystem". This polysystemic approach, which has been heralded with a great deal less fanfare than has deconstructionism, is today gaining more and more adherence in the West as a framework for explaining what takes place in the literary culture. Making use of insights from the field of general systemics, the study of how systems work, Even-Zohar and his colleagues have posited that "literature" in a given society is a collection of various systems, a system-of-systems or polysystem, in which diverse genres, schools, tendencies, and what have you are constantly jockeying for position, competing with each other for readership, but also for prestige and power. Seen in this light, "literature" is no longer the stately and fairly static thing it tends to be for the canonists, but a highly kinetic situation in which things are constantly changing.

Think for a moment of the history of Western literature, for instance since the Renaissance, the way that not only texts, but whole genres and entire movements, emerge, fight their way to the top, then drop back to a secondary or tertiary position, and eventually die. The explanatory power of this polysystemic framework at once becomes obvious.

It also becomes obvious, in a way never accentuated in the traditional literary histories, how central a role literary translations have always played in that highly dynamic macro-system of polysystems that Western literature has been. The spread throughout Europe of such disparate literary elements as the Italian sonnet form, French classicism, or writers like Dostoevsky and Ibsen, for instance, has been almost entirely a consequence of translations. In such situations, the Tel Aviv scholars point out, translations have occupied an innovative, *primary* position, introducing into a literary polysystem new ideas, new methods, new ways of looking at literature and the world, that were not present in it before. In a second phase such elements are imitated and integrated, as native writers take them over in their own "original" writings.

Not all translations have such a function, of course, and much of what you and I spend our time in re-creating is doomed to play only a *secondary* role, complementing and supplementing the existing picture, adjusting it slightly perhaps, but not enough to upset the system. Scholars doing research within the polysystemic framework posit, in fact, that the two kinds of translations, in their ideal forms, have quite different characteristics. In major ways secondary translations conform to the receiving polysystem's notions of what literary texts, or at least translations, should be like, as far as the translations themselves are concerned in their form and style, but also in the concepts, ideas, and themes they present and the ways they present them.

Primary translations, on the other hand, are surprisingly, even shockingly deviant from what they are expected to be, both in the concepts, ideas, and themes taken over from their originals and in their own form and style. It goes without saying, then, that many translations with primary potential in fact never get made, because the translator despairs beforehand of finding a publisher for them, or if they do get made — and published — disappear into oblivion because the gap between their reality and polysystem expectations is really too great to be bridged. In a very few cases their time comes later.

It is clear, then, that the polysystemic approach opens up new vistas. For literary studies first of all, but also for translation studies and, not least of all, the practising literary translator, who can gain from it a clearer insight into the ways in which what he or she is doing functions within the general literary scheme of things.

For one who has taken it upon himself to survey the state of things in translation studies, I have up to now made surprisingly little mention of translation scholars. The fact is that, though schools and university institutes in the Western world have been producing academically-trained translators for over half a century, only the first, hesitant steps have been taken in a very few places towards producing young people with the core of their academic training focused squarely on making them into translation scholars. Twenty years ago there was not even a name for the discipline in most Western languages. All there was, was a somewhat wild-eyed band of scholars, some in general or applied linguistics, some in literary studies, the odd one out in psychology, religion, or cybernetics, who had this thing about translation. Most of us were process-oriented, intrigued by what took place as people performed this strange business of feeding a text in one language into themselves and somehow excreting a strangely similar text in another language. We did our best to observe, to ruminate, and to capture it all in rules, models, flow charts.

Since then, the band has grown, split into camps, held colloquia and conferences, and almost become accepted. There is a certain amount of basic agreement on what our objects of research are, a kind of disciplinary utopia, though some still emphasize the translation process, while others have shifted their major interest to the products of that process and ways to describe them or, a step further, to the functioning of those products in the target culture.

There is one major issue that has split the band down the middle. Many of those who consider themselves translation scholars are, as teachers in translator-training institutes in Western Europe or in translation workshops in America, confronted with the need to provide students with rules or norms, in the straightforward form of: Do this and not that. Others, more empirically and/or historically oriented, tend to reject such a normative point of view as inimical to the scientific method. The controversy has raged furious, particularly in the Low Countries. It is, of course, easily solved. For teachers training translators, operating in the field of applied translation studies, it is a major task to impart norms to students, for they must acquire the skills to function in today's society. But they must also function in tomorrow's, and since even a brief excursion across linguistic borders or incursion into translation history is enough to demonstrate how *hic et nunc* those norms are, it is also a part of the teacher's task to instil in his students an awareness of their relativity ... And perhaps to point out that, in polysystemic terms, those rare translations that come to occupy primary as opposed to secondary positions in the polysystem are frequently precisely the ones that, instead of conforming to the norms, take pride in breaking them.

For those who now think of themselves as translation scholars are not primarily concerned with the day-to-day problems of training young translators, and have come from a background in literary studies, the attraction of the polysystem approach is strong. The result has been that a number of such scholars are now doing exciting research, no longer only in Israel, but also in the Low Countries, England, and the United States, that could change the face of literary history, with the role of translating and translations within that history for the first time really coming into its own.

But at the same time this means that their energies are not being focused on some of the other aspects of translation studies that are vital to improving the quality of translator training and the role of the translator in today's world. We now have a much better model of the translation process than ten years ago, but we still have very little psychological insight into what really goes on inside the black box of the translator's brain. We now have a better understanding than ten years ago of the ways in which literary translations function within a literary culture, or polysystem if you will, but still not enough to be able to predict to a publisher: This is (or will be) a translation that will change the system. We now know much more than we once did about the nature and characteristics of various kinds of texts, but we still have no international repertory or lexicon listing text kinds and types together with their general characteristics and functions and their structural and stylistic differences according to cultural area. And we now probably have more information than ever before, most of it locked inside the heads of translators, about in-context counterparts in Language B for a given word, phrase, idiom, or cultural element in Language A, but our bilingual dictionaries and grammars are still a disgrace and a despair.

The state of the art of translation studies is better than ever before. It is not good. There is so much still to be done.

For Further Reading

On the position of literary translators in Western Europe, see above all Cora Polet, *The Legal, Ecconomic and Social Position of the Literary Translator in the European Economic Community* ((Brussels:) Commission of the European Communities, 1979; Code Nr. CT K 11/961/79-E; English, French, and Dutch texts available). On the concept of translation studies as a discipline, see pp. 67-80 above. For the proceedings of an early colloquium foreshadowing many of the developments of recent years in literary translation studies, see James S Holmes et al. (eds.), *The Nature of Translation* (The Hague & Paris: Mouton and Bratislava: Publishing House of the Slovak Academy of Sciences, 1970: the Bratislava Colloquium). Itamar Even-Zohar's *Papers in Historical Poetics* (Tel Aviv, 1978) contains several papers setting out the basic contours of his polysystem model. Gideon Toury, a younger colleague of Even-Zohar's at Tel Aviv, discusses a number of basic theoretical points in his *In Search of a Theory of Translation* (Tel Aviv, 1980). Finally, at three related colloquia on the study of literary translation and literary intercommunication (in Leuven in 1976, in Tel Aviv in 1978, and in Antwerp in 1980), a number of papers were presented which have been seminal for recent developments. The proceedings of the three colloquia have been issued in the three following collections: James S Holmes et al. (eds.), *Literature and Translation: New Perspectives in Literary Studies* (Leuven: Acco, 1978); Itamar Even-Zohar & Gideon Toury (eds.), *Translation Theory and Intercultural Relations* (Tel Aviv, 1981: a special issue of the review *Poetics Today*, 2, No. 4); and André Lefevere (ed.), "Theory and Translation", pp. 3-179 of *The Art and Science of Translation* (Ann Arbor, Michigan, 1982: a special issue of *Dispositio*, 7, No. 19-21). But the best book of all to start with, as a brief introduction to various approaches to the study of literary translation and translations, is Susan Bassnett-McGuire's *Translation Studies* (London: Methuen, 1980).

Index of Names

Achterberg, 59-61
Agamemnon, 21
Andreas Divus, 33
Apollinaire, Guillaume (pseud. of Guillaume Apollinaire de Kostrowitsky), 14
Arbor, Ann, 43
Arnold, Matthew, 32
Arrowsmith, William, 52
Auden, Wystan Hugh, 14-15, 20

Bacon, Francis, 77, 80
Bailey, Richard Weld, 43
Barnes, Barry P., 79
Barnouw, Adriaan Jacob, 62
Barthes, Roland, 18, 23-24, 30
Bassnett-McGuire, Susan, 111
Baudelaire, Charles Pierre, 83, 85
Bausch, Karl-Richard, 70, 80
Benn, Gottfried, 10, 18
Bridges, Robert Seymour, 43
Brockway, James, 62
Broeck, Raymond van den, 1-5, 80, 91
Brower, Reuben Arthur, 14, 19, 20, 42, 52, 80
Bühler, Hildegund, 103
Bühler, Karl, 75-76, 91
Burnshaw, Stanley, 58

Cary, Henry Francis, 28
Catford, John Cunnison, 18, 31, 42-43
Catullus, Gaius Valerius, 2
Champion, Pierre, 43
Charles d'Orléans, 36-41, 43-44
Chatman, Seymour Benjamin, 51
Chomsky, Noam, 105
Cicero, Marcus Tullius, 31, 93
Circe, 29
Corder, Stephen Pit, 80
Croce, Bendetto, 10, 18
Čukovskij, Kornej Ivanovič, 99

Dante Alighieri, 28
Darbelnet, Jean Louis, 93
Dickens, Charles John Huffam, 103

Dolet, Estienne, 3
Doležel, Lubomír, 43
Dostoevsky, Fedor Mikhailovič, 108
Dryden, John, 19, 24, 31

Eco, Umberto, 104
Egeraat, Leonardus Sebastianus van, 46
Eliot, Thomas Stearns, 20, 33
Ellis, Jeffrey, 31, 33
Even-Zohar, Itamar, 4, 107, 110-113
Ewart, Gavin Buchanan, 39-41

Fitzgerald, Robert Stuart, 29, 33
Fox, John Howard, 43
Frost, Robert Lee, 18
Frost, William, 11, 18

Garvin, Paul Lucian, 43
Geyl, Pieter Catharinus Arie, 62
Goethe, Johann Wolfgang von, 12-13, 19
Goffin, Roger, 69, 80
Goodrich, Norma Lorre, 43
Grierson, Herbert John Clifford, 62
Groom, Bernard, 43
Gunzenhäuser, Rul, 20

Haan, Frans F. de, 19, 52
Haas, William, 32
Hagstrom, Warren O., 67-68, 79-80
Halliday, Michael Alexander Kirkwood, 31
Harris, Roy, 51
Hempel, Carl Gustav, 71, 80
Herreweghen, Hubert Felix Arthur van, 16-18, 21
Hinz, Stella M., 19
Hirschman, Jack, 62
Homer, 25-30, 32-33
Hoornik, Eduard Jozef Antonie Marie, 2, 61
Horguelin, Paul A., 92

Ibsen, Henrik, 108

Jacque, Valentina, 32
Jager, Marjolijn de, 62
Jakobson, Roman, 18, 32, 35, 42, 51, 80, 91
Johnson, Samuel, 48, 51

Khan, Adam, 38-41
Klegraf, Josef, 70, 80
Koller, Werner, 71, 80
Komissarov, Vilen Naumovič, 91, 99
Koptilov, Viktor Viktorovič, 99
Kreuzer, Helmut, 20
Kristeva, Julia, 51

Lambert, José, 82, 89, 91
Lattimore, Richmond Alexander, 28-30, 32-33
Leech, Geoffrey Neil, 38, 43
Lefevere, André Alphons, 3, 51, 91, 98, 111
Levenson, Christopher René, 62
Levý, Jiří, 4, 11, 14, 18-20, 32, 39, 42, 51, 96, 107
Linnaeus, Carolus, 90
Logue, Christopher, 29
Lucebert (pseud. of Lubertus Jacobus Swaanswijk), 58-59
Luther, Martin, 3

MacFarlane, John, 18, 31
Marle, Hans (= Adrianus) van, 2, 62
Martial (Marcus Valerius Martialis), 2
Mathews, Jackson, 12, 19
Mulkay, Michael Joseph, 67, 79
Murry, John Middleton, 31-32

Newman, Francis William, 32
Nicholson, G.R., 40-41, 44
Nida, Eugene Albert, 18, 42-43, 69, 80, 82, 91
Nijhoff, Martinus, 1, 45-46, 49, 51, 55-58, 105
Nijmeijer, Wim Peter, 63

Osers, Ewald, 97
Ostaijen, Paul (= Leopoldus Andreas) van, 14, 19-20
Ovid (Publius Ovidius Naso), 31

Parkinson, George Henry Radcliffe, 32

Poirion, Daniel, 43
Polet, Cora (pseud. of Cora Minnema-Appel), 110
Pope, Alexander, 27
Popovič, Anton, 4, 19, 51-52, 93, 103
Pound, Ezra Loomis, 29-30, 33, 48

Rabin, Chaim, 13, 20
Revius, Jacobus, 63
Revzin, Isaak Iosifovič, 99
Richards, Ivor Armstrong, 73, 80, 104
Rodger, Alexander, 31
Rollins, Scott, 6
Rosenzweig, Franz, 3
Rowlett, Peter, 40-41
Rozencvejg, Viktor Julievič, 99

Sandburg, Carl, 53
Sapir, Edward, 105
Schuur, Koos (= Jacobus), 62
Sebeok, Thomas Albert, 91
Shakespeare, William, 28
Shattuck, Roger, 52
Simmons, Lucretia Van Tuyl, 19
Snoek, Paul (pseud. of Edmond André Coralie Schietekat), 15-17, 20-21, 60-63
Spenser, Edmund, 43
Spilka, Irène, 19
Steele, Robert Reynolds, 43
Steiner, Thomas Robert, 3

Tasso, Torquato, 26
Ten Harmsel, Henrietta, 63
Ten Harmsel, Larry, 63
Tervoort, Bernard Theodoor Marie, 66
Todorov, Tsvetan, 51
Tomaševskij, Boris Viktorovič, 51
Toper, Pavel Maksimovič, 93
Toury, Gideon, 96, 111
Trakl, Georg, 14
Tytler, Alexander Fraser, 3, 32

Ure, Jean M., 31

Van Ameyden van Duym, Hidde, 19
Vanderauwera, Ria, 98
Vasalis, M. (pseud. of Margaretha Droogleever Fortuyn-Leenmans), 58

Verweij, Albert, 15
Vinay, Jean-Paul, 93
Vondel, Joost van den, 15

Watson, George, 31
Weber, Max, 32
Wellek, René, 30
Whorf, Benjamin Lee, 105
Wilss, Wolfram, 70, 79-80
Wright, Arthur Frederick, 80